People Like Us

To all the strong women who came before us

People Like Us

JAN BROWN

Disclaimer

This book is a fictional story based on real people,
places and events. For narrative purposes the book
also contains some fictionalised characters, scenes
and changes to the timing of some events.

First impression: 2022
© Jan Brown & Y Lolfa Cyf., 2022

Cover image: Sion Ilar

ISBN: 978 1 80099 183 5

The publishers wish to acknowledge the support of
Cyngor Llyfrau Cymru

Published and printed in Wales
on paper from well-maintained forests by
Y Lolfa Cyf., Talybont, Ceredigion SY24 5HE
e-mail ylolfa@ylolfa.com
website www.ylolfa.com
tel 01970 832 304
fax 832 782

Gregynog Hall

Prologue

IF I HADN'T made the decision to return to Wales to live, this book would never have been written. Had I not flicked through the pages of the *Welsh Border Life* magazine and noticed an article about Gregynog Hall, giving details of an open afternoon, I would have known nothing about this amazing woman, my great-grandmother, Margaret Davies, known to all who loved her as Gally.

On the many journeys I had made along the A483 through Powys I had seen the small sign just north of Newtown indicating a turn to Gregynog but giving no further information as to what this place might be. Seeing it then in the magazine I discovered a handsome black-and-white property with a long and chequered history, currently owned and managed by the University of Wales. It looked interesting and was only a half-hour car journey from where my husband and I had moved to our new home. Thinking that an afternoon out would be pleasant and well deserved after the house move and ensuing weeks of sorting and unpacking, I booked the tickets.

A fortnight later, we wound our way along narrow country lanes before finding the imposing gates to Gregynog Hall. A long tree-lined drive took us through the estate, and we arrived at the side of the hall, parking next to an old stable block. As it was a lovely September day, we explored the grounds, which had a slightly faded grandeur to them, and enjoyed the many ancient trees surrounding the property. After lunch we made our way to the open afternoon event, starting from the main doors, which were opened at precisely two o'clock.

Our group was quite large, and we were almost the last to cross the threshold. As I walked into a roomy lobby, I had one of those déjà vu moments. I said nothing, listening instead to the history that our guide was relaying. However, as we started to move along the corridor, my mind switched off from his words and I began to feel evermore certain of what I was going to see in the next room. These feelings continued throughout the house tour, and at one moment I found myself pointing in the direction of where the kitchens would be, and becoming certain that the final room downstairs would be a small sitting room, which it was.

None of these feelings were at all frightening; if anything, I felt really comfortable, and experienced a sense of being at home throughout the property. We were given permission to go upstairs and wander the first-floor landing, bedrooms and bathrooms. Here, again, there was a sense of familiarity, much as I had felt in childhood when I would stay with relatives whom we only saw periodically. I knew the house but felt the need to familiarise myself again with the details. Over tea afterwards, I shared my feelings with my husband. I had no actual memory of having been here before, but as the place is only some forty miles from my childhood home, it was possible that I had come here as a girl with my parents. This seemed the logical explanation.

As soon as we arrived home, I called my father to ask him if he had ever taken me there. Dad is ninety-four but mentally very sharp. His reply was somewhat cagey, although he was adamant that he had never taken me to Gregynog. When I had started relaying the events of the afternoon, he dropped a bombshell.

'Your great-grandparents were in service there. Your great-grandmother was the cook in the late 1800s and your great-grandfather was the carter. There's quite a story about it all.'

I felt the hairs on the back of my neck stand up, quickly becoming certain that this story was one that I had no choice but to follow, wherever it may lead me. So began my research with family, librarians, local historians, the internet and the National Library of Wales. The latter provided me with an opportunity to turn the pages of the Gregynog Estate records from the 1800s and see the wages paid to my ancestors and the rent paid by them to the various owners of the house. All of these experiences embedded in me a deep respect and affection for this strong, capable and loving woman: Gally.

Although I have been fortunate to have been able to spend many hours with my father and aunt, who were both cared for during their childhood by Gally, and so have many small and intimate memories which I have included whenever appropriate, it is impossible to build a completely accurate picture of the past, and because of that some events have been created or moved slightly to add to the story. All events that occurred at Gregynog have been reported faithfully, using local history books and reference material.

What follows is a depiction of the life and times as seen through the eyes of my great-grandmother as she played out her role as an ordinary woman at the turn of the twentieth century in mid Wales.

PART I
1915

Chapter 1

THE STEADY BEAT of the pony's hooves pounded through Margaret's head; the pressure inside her skull had grown with every mile that they had travelled. Pulling her heavy woollen shawl tighter around her head and shoulders, she flicked the reins again, hoping to encourage a faster pace from old Dolly. She knew it would be in vain; Dolly had one speed, and never altered it for anyone. Her three youngest daughters sat on the rear boards of the cart, all their belongings heaped into the space between them and the seat up front. The cart creaked and groaned, the old timbers complaining at the heavy load as they struggled up and down the winding lanes from Tregynon towards Llanidloes.

The journey had taken almost the whole day, and – apart from a quick stop at the edge of Llandinam to rest Dolly, and for them all to share the cold tea and bread and cheese hurriedly wrapped in greaseproof paper before their early departure – the girls had sat together with none of their usual laughter and singing. For the most part they had sat in silence, their high spirits diminished by the events of the last week and replaced with a fear of the unknown. Their young faces were blank with the shock of their father's death and the way in which their lives had been turned upside down.

Margaret, too, was struggling with a mind full of turmoil; the loss of her husband Thomas was a mixed blessing, as he hadn't been an easy man to live with, but he had been a provider and now her immediate concern was for the future. She and the girls were homeless, and she had no job and no means of supporting them all. Margaret was doing what had always seemed the natural thing to do in times of trouble. She was heading home; home to Glan-y-nant and her sisters.

The gentle rhythm of the pony's hooves allowed her thoughts to wander, and she recalled the day of Thomas' funeral.

*

As the mourners had started to leave the family's home after the funeral tea, a tall figure had filled the doorway. It was Mr Scott Owen, the estate manager from Gregynog Hall. Seeing him there at her own front door, she had known that there was more bad news coming her way. She had braced her shoulders, stiffened her spine and welcomed him over the threshold. The last few people quietly said their farewells and quit the house, leaving her alone with her visitor.

'Mrs Owens, I do apologise for not being able to attend the service for Thomas; I had a meeting with Lord Davies. There are to be a great many changes on the estate. I have to give you this, with much regret.'

He pressed her hand whilst handing her a sealed official envelope.

Throughout the day Margaret had masked her anger and fears, but now her emotions erupted and she felt incapable of speech. Deep down, she had known that this moment would arrive – she had seen it happen to others – but she had imagined a little time would pass for them to recover from the shock of Thomas' death.

It was only six days since she had found him dead in their marriage bed. He had not followed her downstairs as he usually did in the morning, and, after preparing his porridge and placing it on the sturdy scrubbed table, she had climbed the stairs to shake him awake. Those of the men who had not joined the war effort were left with a very heavy workload, since there were fewer of them; indeed, the number employed on the estate had fallen to its lowest ever. Margaret guessed that Thomas had simply fallen back into a deep sleep. She had not been prepared for the stillness in the small bedroom; a total absence of any sound of breathing told her at once that he had gone. Still, she had touched his cheek to find it still warm, and so followed a natural instinct by shaking his shoulder, gently at first – for he was not a man to cross – and then with increasing urgency, before accepting the truth.

Crossing to her daughters' room, she had woken Peggy and urged her to run quickly to find her uncle John, who would already be hard at work outside, wondering where Thomas was. Within minutes, he had come in from the cold December morning and – seeing her face – had climbed the narrow stairs to see for himself. There followed a flurry of activity, breaking the news to the three girls, sending for old Dr Williams so that the death could be registered and arrangements made for a simple funeral service in Bethany Chapel. The days had passed in a blur of work, for all Thomas' tasks had to be done as well as the usual household chores.

Margaret and her daughters had worked tirelessly to feed the livestock, break the ice on the well and the water troughs and chop firewood. Thomas, meanwhile, had lain in a wooden coffin on trestles in the small front parlour, the curtains drawn and one candle constantly lit. Exhausted by the end of every day, she had simply fallen onto the bed where she had found her dead husband, sleeping soundly until the next day began. There had been no time for grief, between working and consoling the girls, especially Ellen, the youngest. There had simply been no space for her to give voice to her own thoughts and feelings.

The sight of that letter from the estate manager acted as a catalyst. Saying nothing, she had simply held open the door and watched as Mr Scott Owen doffed his hat before leaving.

Margaret had slumped into a chair and torn open the envelope. A week's grace! She and the girls were to be evicted from their tied cottage. Just a week after all the years that she and Thomas had worked for Lord Joicey and before him, Lord Sudeley! All those hours in the hot steaming kitchens, preparing endless meals for banquets and parties, for celebrations and weddings, her skill with pastry and desserts, her long hours bent over white cotton sheets with her needle as she created the most delicate of stitches to repair tears and small holes – none of this counted for anything.

There had been so many changes at the hall, especially inside, since no family was in residence and it was increasingly dedicated to shooting parties. Margaret had hoped, now that Lord Davies had bought the estate, that things would change for the better, but it seemed as though loyalty and hard work counted for nothing. She had a week to pack her things and she, Peg, Polly and Ellen would have to leave Lower Cefntwlch.

Anger and indignation burned inside her: anger at Thomas for having a heart attack, anger at a world that allowed people like her to be treated in this way, to have no rights, no future. Most of all, she felt anger at herself, for ever being tempted to marry; she should have known that married life would never work out for her. Why had she abandoned her hard-won independence, her status as cook at Gregynog Hall, the life she had created through her own hard work. She had lost all this when she married Thomas, the estate carter, the handyman, the labourer. As her tears began to fall, she realised that she was not alone. A hand crept round her shoulders and she felt the comfort of her daughters wrap around her. Her five children were what she had gained, and she could never regret them, they had always brought her such joy and comfort. Sarah, the eldest, working away at Connah's Quay in the munitions' factory, son Thomas serving his country in this dreadful war, and the three youngest still here with her. She had taken a deep breath, smiled at her girls and sent them to change before attending to the outside tasks. Megan must be milked, the poultry shut away before dark and the pony fed and watered and brought in to the small stable. Being busy would be good for them.

Pulling on an old sacking apron over her Sunday best dress, Margaret had set to in her kitchen. The fine china cups were washed and returned to the dresser, crumbs from the Welsh cakes and Bara Brith swept from the stone floor as she vented her frustration on inanimate objects until the everyday actions and routines began to restore her usual calm demeanour. There would be no Christmas celebrations for the Owens family in 1915, there was simply too much to do over the next seven days.

The week had passed, the animals had been sold, her cherished items of furniture from the front parlour sold back to old Mr Watkins in Llanfair Caereinion, their meagre belongings packed, letters sent to Sarah and Thomas to inform them of their father's death and that she and the girls were returning to Llanidloes.

Their journey was nearing its end, and – as they dropped down the hill into Llanidloes – the light was fading and gas lamps and candles had already been lit in the smart houses where the *crachach* lived. Determined not to be seen as an object of pity, Margaret straightened her tired shoulders, lifted her head and clicked again at the reins, urging Dolly to trot smartly along Broad Street. There were still ladies returning from the shops who noticed the small pony and trap and the three girls sitting at the back with their eyes cast down. Margaret looked straight ahead, acknowledging no one and keeping her eyes fixed firmly on the road ahead. News of her widowhood would have spread, carried by the farmers at market and the travelling salesmen and – although she was pleased to be home where she felt safe and comfortable – she knew that there would be some in the town who would welcome her downfall. The lives of some of her school friends had not turned out well, and many had been jealous of her position at the big house in Tregynon. Now they would be having a field day at her misfortune.

A final turn across the bridge, over the Severn, just as the siren sounded to call an end to the day's work at the woollen mill, and the little cart left the lights of the town behind and began the final climb to the hamlet of Glan-y-nant.

Chapter 2

Dᴜʀɪɴɢ ᴛʜᴇ ɴɪɢʜᴛ a hard frost had fallen, coating even the inside of the small window pane of the tiny bedroom. The patchwork quilt had slipped from her shoulders and, as she began to wake, Margaret became aware of how cold she felt. She tugged at the bed covers to lift them back into place, and was shocked to realise that there was someone else in her bed. The regular sound of someone breathing roused her to a wide-awake state, and thoughts tumbled through her mind as she readjusted her mental compass. It could not be Thomas; she was in fact sharing a bed with Peg. The sound she could hear was the Severn rushing down through the valley, only feet away from where she lay. The previous day's journey played out again in her head and she lay still, not wanting to wake her daughter, needing some time and space to come to terms with all that had happened.

*

When they had finally arrived at her sister's small cottage, there had been a warm welcome from Lizzie and her husband Jack. The second bedroom in the eaves of the cottage had been cleared of clutter, and the bed made up for her and Peg, whilst the old bed against the wall in the kitchen had been readied for the two younger girls. Polly and Ellen had loved the idea of slipping in to the warm bed, so close to the fireplace, and then drawing the curtain across to give them a secret hideaway. They had all been fed with heaped plates of warming *cawl*, the leeks and carrots steaming hot, the mutton stewed to tenderness and all the juice wiped clean with slices of Lizzie's freshly-made bread. Somehow, things had not seemed quite so bad with a full stomach and thoughts of a cosy bed and the comforting common sense of her younger sister.

'It is what it is Margaret, and you and the girls can stay as long as you need to. It'll sort itself out. It usually does and He never sends us more than we can cope with. Go and rest and see what the morning brings.'

PART II
1871

Chapter 3

MEMORIES OF HER childhood coursed through her subconscious as she lay in a deep sleep, memories that brought comfort as she relived them. Summer days were always the best, remembered fondly for their long hours and freedom from the chilblains which troubled her so in the cold winter months. This year they had been blessed with long hot days to ripen the corn and wheat, and just enough rain to ensure a good crop of vegetables and fruit. Young as she was, Margaret had worked alongside her mother, preparing fruit for bottling, peeling and slicing beans for salting, and laying carrots and potatoes in old sacks ready for the vegetable store outside. The arched recess, a brick-lined construction going far back into the hill, was a great place to play in the spring as it emptied of produce.

Margaret and her mother left the house at dawn – walking as quickly as the little girl's legs would allow – and headed for the field at the bottom of the hill. The long grass, soaked in early morning dew, wet their legs. Hanging from the hedges were intricate spiders' webs glistening in the sunshine. Early mornings in late summer were a magical time, and the wild mushrooms were lying in the meadow as if they had been waiting for their hands to come and pluck them. Her mother Meg knew which ones to choose and which to leave behind, and now that Margaret was five years old, she was beginning to know the best ones to look for. Once they had filled their flat basket, they began the walk back up the hill, watching the sun rise behind the house and the mist slowly leaving the valley.

'What's wrong, Mam?' Margaret asked as they walked. 'Are you hurting?'

Her mother had grimaced and pressed her hand into the small of her back. There was to be another baby soon – that much young Margaret had guessed – and her mother took her hand and gave a smile of reassurance.

'Best we get home Margaret; I think you may have another brother or sister before too long.'

After a breakfast of fried mushrooms and bread and butter, Margaret had cleared away the dishes and set her younger sisters to play outside. She sat with her mother, watching her face crease with pain and knowing that soon her grandmother would arrive to help and she would be able to escape outside with the others. Her father had been gone for some time now, so soon they should hear the rattle of the cart as it came down the stony track, bringing the comforting presence of her *nain*. It was always the role of the older women to act as midwives; they provided the only help for most women in childbirth. Once the baby was safely delivered she would be back home to tend to her own duties.

By early evening, her brother Richard was born, a tiny scrap with a shock of dark hair, named after his father and welcomed with huge pleasure as the first boy in the family and someone to carry on life at Cancoed. The house had originally been a *tŷ unnos*, a house built in one night on common land by Richard's grandfather. In order to stake a claim to such a home, four walls, a roof and smoke coming through an opening had to be constructed overnight. Since then, the house had been replaced with the current building. Although it was still a squat and simple construction, it was sturdily built of stone, and had a tiled roof. The house seemed to have been a part of the landscape for ever.

Upstairs there were three bedrooms, the largest for her parents and now little Richard for a while, one for the two younger girls, Lizzie and Ann, and a small room tucked right under the eaves and above the kitchen, where Margaret slept by herself. She loved this tiny room; there was barely room to walk around her little iron bed, but the space was hers, and here she would play with her one wooden doll, read her two books, both gifts from the Sunday school teacher Miss Evans, when she had seen how much Margaret loved to read. The pages had already been worn at the edges when she had been given them, but the two stories of Daniel and Noah – illustrated in pen and ink – were Margaret's most prized possessions. She loved the little school at Glan-y-nant, never minding the two mile walk each way. Her heart had fallen a little at the news of Richard's birth, as she knew that there would be no school for her for the next week or so until her mam was back on her feet.

Downstairs, there were two main rooms. One was the parlour, never used except on Sunday afternoons in winter and on special occasions; woe betide the children if they were ever caught entering without permission. Margaret had sometimes seen her mother standing at the open door and just looking in, a small smile on her face as she gazed at the hard-earned trophies of upright chairs, a few china ornaments, the ticking wall clock and the woollen rug before the tiled fireplace. It was not a comfortable room for a child to be in, no playthings or books were allowed and Margaret found it agony to be told to sit in there at any time. She much preferred the warmth and muddle of the other room, the kitchen. Here there was no fancy rug, just the herringbone pattern of the stones which her paternal grandmother had collected from the fields and then laid to make the floor. Here there was noise and laughter, singing and chatter, wonderful smells from stews and pies, and bread baking in the old oven above the fireplace. This was the heart of her home and the place where Margaret felt safest; she never minded the chores, the trips outside in mid-winter to the chilly *tŷ bach*, the repetitive pattern of the days, months and seasons. Her childhood was a simple one, regular schooling unless she was needed at home, weekly visits to chapel and Sunday school, hours spent playing outdoors in the fields and meadows, running along the riverbank, trying in vain to catch young trout. As she had grown, the balance had swung from play to work and she had become almost as good in the kitchen as her mother, could help birth a lamb, kill and pluck a chicken, milk the cow and harness up the trap. Margaret had taken to all these activities with willingness and a cheerful nature, and was most times to be found singing as she worked, the Welsh hymns she had learned at chapel filling the kitchen with her clear voice.

There were more children by the time Margaret was thirteen, and the house was bursting at the seams, with the youngest two now having to sleep on truckle beds in the corner of the kitchen. Perhaps she should have been prepared for what came next but she had never been one for looking to the future, she just enjoyed each day. After their evening meal, her father asked her to sit down with him at the table. She had felt worried, thinking that she had done something wrong and was to be reprimanded, a rare thing indeed. But her father had more sobering news.

'Margaret, you are to be leaving us next Thursday. You can see how it is here, the house is too full, and it's time you earned a living.'

'Where will I go? What about school?'

He had taken her hand in his work-roughened and scarred hand before continuing, 'At market last week, I met a farmer, David Williams, from Trefeglwys, and they are looking for a girl to help in the house and on the farm, work such as you do here. His wife has just had twins and is not able to do all the chores as before. You can do the work easily, and it is time for Lizzie to take your place. He will pay you £3 a year and you will have four days off each year when you will be able to come home and see us. There is to be no more school for you, Margaret; you are grown up now and must take your place in the world.'

This had been a long speech for her father, a man of few words. He had placed his hand on her shoulder before heading off outside to see to the animals, leaving Margaret to deal with her feelings. Tears fell down her cheeks as she looked around her at all that was dear to her, the clothes hanging above the fire to air, the dishes carefully stacked on the oak dresser, the old settle where she sat on a winter's evening to sew with her mother. She didn't want to leave it all.

The door creaked as her mother came down the stairs and in to the kitchen. Seeing her daughter's face, she said, 'He's told you then?'

Margaret nodded and her mother had sat next to her, stroking her hair back as she had when she was a small child.

'It has to be, Margaret. You cannot stay here for ever. You

have to make a life now and at least you will not be too far away and we shall see you every year. You will be fine, and there will be children to care for and you know how good you are with little ones. You will have a small room for yourself, and Mr Williams has promised that you will go to chapel with them on Sundays.'

Chapter 4

Dawn was just breaking as Margaret had sat on the side of her bed, watching the view from her tiny window for what felt as though it would be the last time ever. She had not slept at all after the efforts of staying cheerful the previous evening, her heart lying like a heavy suet pudding between her ribs. Mam had made her favourite rabbit stew followed by a golden apple and blackberry tart, but there had been no taste in her mouth, no pleasure in her soul. The last week had been a succession of farewells, to her friends at chapel, her teacher, Mr Harris, who had shaken her hand and urged her to keep reading, to her grandparents, to the animals on the farm (especially Sian the cow and Dick the pony), and now this morning she would have to leave her younger brothers and sisters and her mam, as Dad took her down to Llanidloes in the cart where they would meet Mr Wiliams at the market and then she would be gone, away over the hills to this faraway place called Trefeglwys! Margaret had never been further than the centre of Llanidloes, five miles away from where she was sitting right then, and the thought of leaving all that was dear and familiar to her, was terrifying. She would be alone, far from everyone she knew! Again she felt her stomach contract in fear and anxiety, and knew that she would have to tiptoe down the stairs and out to the privy again.

Her father threw her small bag onto the cart along with

the sacks of vegetables and Mam's butter and eggs for their regular market pitch, and climbed on to the seat. Dick stamped his hooves, ready for off. With a final hug, Mam had pushed her away and there had been nothing else to do but climb up alongside her father. Tears had misted her eyes and her face was deathly white as they turned their backs on the little stone house and started off up the lane. Margaret had turned her head for one last look at her family but already her Mam had been urging the children inside; they would need to be fed before going to school, and for Lizzie the day marked her taking over all the chores that had been Margaret's. They had no time to stand waving her off. She understood, but somehow it felt as if she had already been forgotten. As they drew closer to town, there were more carts and more people walking in the direction of the market, women laden with baskets of eggs, beautifully formed butter pats, each with their own distinctive pattern stamped on the top, carts loaded with hens and ducks, sacks of potatoes and swedes, carrots and cabbages, apples and plums. Margaret had only ever been a few times before, and now the excitement of seeing so much activity took over and her natural sense of optimism began to resurface.

'Look at all the sheep, there in the road, Dad, how will we get by?'

''Tis always like that, Margaret, they pen them up in Great Oak Street so that everyone can look at the animals, and then Thomas the auctioneer will take his stand right outside the Trewythen, and the sale will begin. We can take a look once we've found a pitch.'

At the top of the street, her father's usual spot was free, so he slowed the cart, gave Dick his bucket of bran and unloaded his goods onto the road. People were arriving in larger numbers now; even though it was still before eight the best items were soon chosen and hurried away with. The chatter and banter between sellers and customers soon had Margaret smiling and she forgot her fears as she helped her father fill the baskets of the women with her mother's eggs and butter, the vegetables she had helped to pick and the apples from the old tree by the stable at Cancoed. Their goods were almost gone when a deep voice cried out, 'Davies, man, be this your daughter, then?' Margaret's fear had returned in an instant, and the temperature dropped, leaving her shivering in her newly-washed summer dress.

'It is Williams,' her father answered. 'Come here, Margaret, and make yourself known. Mr Williams is to be your employer now and you must work hard and do all he and his wife ask of you.'

He had drawn Margaret forward and she had stood silently, taking in this new person who would play a big role in her new life.

'Good Morning, sir,' had been all that she could manage in a quiet voice. In a matter of minutes, her father had passed her bag to her, patted her shoulder kindly and she was being led away down through the crowds, past the livestock, around the old market hall and towards the Angel. Mr Williams hadn't spoken a word directly to her but he was a large man and walked quickly and with purpose, leaving her scuttling along behind him, burdened with her bag. As they reached the inn, he turned to her and motioned to the bench under the tree.

'Sit there while I go in for some food. I'll send some out for you and then we'll be off.'

Within minutes, a young girl appeared from the rear of the inn with a cup of milk and a slice of fresh bread, amply spread with salted butter. Margaret took the food gratefully as she had refused breakfast at home, but now she wondered when her next meal would be. Her youthful resilience and curiosity had revived somewhat, and as she enjoyed her simple meal she started to look around her. Certainly, many men were heading inside the inn, clearly country folk, but their clothing less threadbare and their boots less worn than her own father's. Many knew each other and called out greetings and comments about the weather and the harvest. There were few women to be seen in this part of town, although occasionally one would walk quickly down the street with a laden basket, heading home from market to begin the day's chores. The lane leading to the Angel seemed to be almost reserved for men, and Margaret wondered what her mam would make of seeing her daughter left sitting here. As she finished her bread, drank the last of the creamy milk and wiped the remnants from around her mouth with the back of her hand, she became aware that she was being watched, just as she had been watching what was going on around her. Two young men were walking unsteadily from the inn and began to amble towards her. Margaret sat upright, her hands on the bag on her knees, and looked into the distance. What was she to do if they spoke to her?

Before that could happen, Mr Williams came through the door, shouting at the lads to clear off and leave her alone and for the first time Margaret was glad of his protection.

'Young 'uns can't hold their ale. Didn't bother you, did they?'

'No, sir, and thank you for the bread and milk. I was hungry.'

'Well, miss, 'tis Margaret we must call you, your father

29

says? I shall get my trap from the stable behind and then we'll be off.'

Within minutes, both she and her small bag – containing all she owned in the world – were stowed onto the trap, Mr Williams gave a flick of the reins and his shiny black horse trotted swiftly out into the street and out of town.

Chapter 5

THEY HAD BEEN travelling for less than an hour when the
village of Trefeglwys came into sight. Before Margaret
could get more than a glimpse of a row of stone cottages and
the church spire, Mr Williams had turned the horse sharply to
the left and they began to climb a steep lane. The hedges were
full of blackberries and hazelnuts, the glowing pink flowers of
the rose bay willow herb long gone to seed, its white whispy
heads a sure sign that autumn had arrived. They passed a
few houses and the gates to farms but the horse and cart kept
moving, the black horse seeming to Margaret to find renewed
energy as he neared the end of his hard day, his stable and a
good feed. In her case, though, arrival spelt the return of her
nerves. What would she find at this new home? Would the
mistress be kind or hard? Would Margaret herself be able to
deal with the work?

The cart turned in through a gate and they were
now approaching a sprawling black-and-white timbered
farmhouse. This was a substantial dwelling with many
outbuildings. Margaret could see both sheep and cattle in
the surrounding fields, and her heart sank at the thought of
being part of such a place. A farm worker standing by the
stable called out to Mr Williams, raised his hand in greeting
and then, to her relief, they were through the yard and
continuing along an even narrower lane. Seeing the look of

fear and apprehension on Margaret's face, her new employer turned to say, 'That's Cefn Barach, a grand farm and our nearest neighbour, but I'm afraid we are a smaller concern than that. Tŷ Uchaf is part of the estate, a rented farm, I am a tenant farmer but my family have been here for three generations and more to come, with God's grace. I hope you will soon settle with us, as my wife is in real need of help. The twins are just a few weeks old and she has been weak since the birth, so things are not as they should be. I am hoping that having you here will help her to recover her strength. Your father said you were good in the house and with the little ones, so it will be up to you to see what needs doing.'

From her perch on the cart, overlooking the surrounding fields, Margaret realised that this new home was going to be far more remote than Cancoed had been. There would be no trips to town here, no escape, except for the weekly trip to chapel with the family. Her spirits lifted as they finally drew to a halt outside a long low building, the walls whitewashed and the roof made from dark grey slates. At the front was a small strip of garden where ragged daisies and stocks looked forlorn and in need of care. To the right of the house stood a large barn, already half-full of hay, two stables with their doors open wide, a pigpen and byre. The yard was full of chickens, and she could hear the rattle of a chain and the repeated barking of a dog somewhere to the rear of the house. As she jumped down from the seat, the front door opened and a young man, more than a boy but not fully a man, stood silently looking in her direction. He said nothing, but his stance was one of ownership: this was where he belonged. Margaret looked back carefully, noticing the small scar on his lower cheek, the open-necked work shirt, loosely tucked inside his trousers. His one hand held his braces and, with the other, he held firmly to the old wooden door. Before either could speak, Mr Williams called out,

'Walter, get your boots on and come help me unload the cart, there's provisions for the house.'

He turned to Margaret, passed her bag across and motioned her towards the door.

'This here is Walter, my son by my first wife. She died many years ago now. It was consumption. In you go now, kitchen is first door on the right and you'll likely find Mrs Williams and the babies in there. I must see to the horse.'

Margaret walked slowly towards the house, nodding to Walter as she passed and walking quickly through the doorway into the gloom of a stone passageway. She knocked, pushed open the door on the right and stood, shocked at the sight before her. Used as she was to her mother's ordered kitchen, always full of cooking smells and freshly laundered clothes, this room left her reeling. There was a meagre fire burning in the grate, a cradle placed next to it and the table was covered in used dishes and plates. It had been many days since the floor had been brushed or washed, and the pervading smell in the room was of dirt, smoke and the strong ammonia of soiled napkins. Sitting in a wooden rocker beside the table was Mrs Williams. She looked up at Margaret's arrival but seemed to have no energy to speak, merely lowering her gaze and shrinking back into her chair. The silence was broken by a cry from one of the babies. Putting down her bag, Margaret crossed the room to the cradle and lifted out the child. His small face was creased with anger, his cries increasing until she blew gently into his face, the surprise causing him to open wide blue eyes and draw in a deep calming breath.

'These babies need feeding and changing, Miss, where are the napkins?'

At this Mrs Williams began to sob quietly. 'I can't do it again. I haven't got enough milk. They're always hungry. I don't know what to do and I'm so tired. The napkins are there in the basket; there aren't many left: they need to be washed but I just can't seem to do it.'

Margaret crossed the room and found two clean cloths, then took a bowl from the dresser and filled it with warm water from the kettle on the stove. Deciding to deal with the little boy first, she washed and changed him, singing throughout the procedure, repeating the words of one of her favourite hymns. She repeated the process with the little girl and laid them again in the cradle before turning to their mother.

'They're beautiful babies, Mrs Williams, you must tell me about them when we have a chance! But they are hungry, right now. Do you have a goat? When my mam couldn't feed her baby, we used goat's milk, it will be fine if we water it down a little to start with. Do you have bottles, bottles for the lambs?'

Mrs Williams seemed to rouse herself, shaken from her exhaustion by Margaret's presence. Having given her directions to find the two goats at the back of the barn, she stood up and went to find the feeding bottles. Margaret took this as a good sign, and quickly set off to find the goats. She had been milking animals since her early childhood and she soon fastened the animals to the post, settled on the milking stool, and quickly filled a pail with creamy milk. By the time she returned, the bottles and teats were ready on the table and she half-filled them with milk as she had seen her mother do and then topped them up with water from the kettle before fixing on the rubber teats. Mrs Williams had sat down again and said nothing, but took one baby and a bottle from Margaret and began to feed the child. Margaret sat opposite, took the second baby, and before long the room was quiet except for the contented sounds of babies sucking.

'What are their names?'

'This is Huw, and you are feeding Gwyneth. How do you know so much about babies?'

'I am the eldest of six; as long as I can remember there has been a baby in our house, and the last few have been hard for Mam, she's been really tired and couldn't always feed them. You need to drink lots of liquid to help your milk. When they have finished, I'll make some tea while you tell me what needs doing.'

Within a few minutes, the two sleeping children were back in the cradle, the kettle was returned to the hob and Margaret stood looking around her.

'Is there supper made, Miss? The men will need a meal before long, and you must eat too, to build yourself up again.'

From her chair, Mrs Williams shook her head, her eyes filling with tears as she confessed that there was nothing ready. Margaret made hot sweet tea for them both before pouring the rest of the hot water in to the old stone sink and making short work of all the dirty dishes. One look in the pantry showed a lack of stores and little in the way of provisions laid down for winter. Back at home, the shelves were already laden with fruit and vegetables, bottled and salted for the winter months to come. There was a bag of onions, a sack of potatoes and on the cold slab butter and cheese. Reaching for the flour from the top shelf, Margaret knew that her only hope was to make a cheese and onion pie. She worked furiously, building up the fire to ensure a hot oven, making pastry as she had so many times at home, grating cheese and slicing onions before finding a deep earthenware dish to hold her pie.

Throughout this busy time, the older woman remained motionless in her chair, her only request, that her teacup be refilled. Soon the heady aroma of the meal began to waft through the kitchen, and just as Margaret had finished sweeping the floor, the door opened and the two men came in.

'My word, girl, you have done wonders in here already, and is that supper cooking? I was only expecting bread and cheese again but whatever that is, it smells wonderful.'

She served the meal to the family, and – dishing up a slice of pie for herself – went to sit at the back of the room.

'No, you must sit here with us, you have worked so hard. Come, sit here, next to me.'

Mrs Williams had found her voice at last, and the colour was returning to her cheeks as she ate the hot and tasty meal. The men cleared their plates, took second helpings and finally sat back, replete after their first hot meal for some time. Margaret stood to clear the dishes and offered more tea, taking care to add extra sugar to her mistress' cup. As she washed the crockery again, she looked around the kitchen and saw that it was a good-sized room, well furnished with solid furniture, table and chairs, a dresser and settle near the fire. The china was good quality, all matching, in a blue-and-white pattern that she knew her mam would love. What was needed here was some order, a few days cleaning and polishing would soon return the room to the way it must have been.

Having finished their meal, the men left to shut away the livestock and attend to the last of the day's chores. The babies had begun to grizzle again, and Margaret felt confident enough to suggest that this time she feed Huw with a bottle while Mrs Williams feed Gwyneth herself. If her milk supply could cope with one child, then they could be alternated between breast and bottle. Mrs Williams agreed to try: she seemed calmer now. But when Margaret handed her the baby and she pulled aside her dress, Margaret was shocked to see that her breast was red and inflamed. The new mother's initial apparent discomfort as the baby began to suckle was genuine pain. Margaret recognised this condition as mastitis; her mother had suffered with this too, and though they had no money to spare for doctors, the girl did remember what had been done to ease the discomfort. When both babies had been fed again and settled, Margaret went into the pantry and, after some searching, found what she wanted: a cabbage. Taking the outer leaves off carefully, she went back and passed them to her mistress.

'You have an infection, Miss, my mam had it too, and she swore by the cabbage leaves. Put them inside your dress, next to your skin on each side, and they will ease the pain.'

For the first time, her new mistress smiled. 'Cabbage leaves? Well, I'll try it, because my breasts are so painful. I think you may be just what we need here! Now tell me, what's your name? What should I call you?'

Chapter 6

TIME PASSED; DAYS grew into weeks, weeks into months. Four years turned with the seasons, and Margaret was now a young woman. She no longer wore her long black hair loose but pulled it back tightly, winding the coils into a firm knot at the back of her head. It should have made her look older and perhaps stern, but the twinkle remained in her indigo eyes and, as the day moved along, tendrils of hair escaped from their binding and softened around her face. Her body had changed, becoming softer and shapely but she was still tall and slender, standing head and shoulders above Mrs Williams now.

The house had also changed. Margaret's presence enabled Mrs Williams to make a full recovery and the garden and kitchen echoed with the singing and laughter of little Huw and Gwyneth. There had been no further additions to the family, and although Margaret had been aware of many cross words spoken in the master and mistress' bedroom – the room lay directly below hers and she could not fail to hear the arguments – Mrs Williams had held hard to her resolve not to repeat the experience of carrying and giving birth to twins. She had become a good friend, allowing Margaret to address her as Miss Flo, which was what Walter called her. The two women now shared the household tasks, working alongside each other as sisters would. The house gleamed, the furniture was polished to a high sheen, the pantry shelves were laden with produce, and the smells of bread baking, roasting meat and spicy meat pies filled the kitchen. Margaret had taken charge of the kitchen garden, and throughout the summer they harvested potatoes and carrots, cabbage and beans, onions and marrows. The apple and plum trees, meanwhile, presented the household with a glut of fruit. The small dairy next to the barn was now back in production, and Margaret churned butter as she had done at Cancoed, making soft goat's cheese and a crumbly, salty white cheese to her mother's old recipe.

She had made three visits home, Mr Williams honouring his promise that she have four days off each year. Margaret had chosen to go on the days around her mother's birthday in May, and the trips had been full of talk and sharing stories, delight at seeing her family and hearing the progress of the little ones. By the third year, however, she was less sad to return to the Williams' farm, having grown accustomed to her new life and enjoying the space around her at Tŷ Uchaf and the free hours in the evenings when she could indulge her love of books. When Mrs Williams had realised that Margaret could read, she had been quick to show her the small selection of books in the parlour and invite her to borrow them. Each year, their small library had grown with books given as Christmas and birthday gifts to both women.

Margaret's relationship with the young man Walter had begun to change. For the first couple of years she had kept her distance, always finding a reason to be elsewhere when he entered the kitchen, walking in the opposite direction should their paths cross outside in the yard or garden. But over the last year, Walter had become more persistent, demanding a response to his comments and questions, drawing her slowly into conversation. The winter evenings forced the family to sit in the same room, to keep warm around the fire. While she tried to concentrate on her book, Margaret could feel his eyes on her as he struggled to complete the farm account books in the dim candlelight. For the last few months, he had manoeuvred his way to sit beside her in chapel on Sundays and she had been aware of his strong thigh pressing against her leg, the rough cloth of his Sunday best suit rubbing at the fine grey wool of her new Sunday dress, a hand-me-down from Mrs Williams, lengthened with a flounce of dark green fabric. On her last visit home, her mother had given her a length of green velvet ribbon, and on Sundays she coiled this in her hair and couldn't help but sneak quick glances at her reflection in the parlour mirror when she was passing.

It was to be expected that she and Walter would be drawn to each other; they were living in a remote spot with little contact with other families, apart from the service on Sunday in Trefeglwys. They were both healthy young creatures with normal desires and feelings, and so the closeness deepened. Whenever she headed to the garden to pull vegetables, he would arrive with a basket. Should she be struggling to peg out heavy white sheets on a windy day, Walter would suddenly appear to put the heavy wooden prop into place. The summer evenings had given them time and opportunity to walk the country lanes. It was then – knowing autumn would be upon them soon and they would be confined to the parlour and the watchful eye of his father – that Walter became more daring. He would reach for her hand to hold, once they were away from the farm, or steal a kiss behind the old oak tree, each small step feeding their affection and desire to be alone.

Young bodies are made for loving and all the dos and don'ts of parents and preachers are soon forgotten in the heat of the moment. Around them the natural world was blooming, trees laden with fruit, fields full of crops, hedges heavy with berries and nuts. It wasn't long before Margaret, too, began to suspect that her body was changing. Retching into the bowl on her small chest of drawers, Margaret shivered in the chilly autumn morning. This was the third day that she had been unwell and she knew that she could no longer blame her stomach upset on eating too much rhubarb or drinking dirty water. She had seen her mother like this on too many occasions not to recognise the truth. She was going to have a child.

Confident that Walter would stand by her, support her and marry her, she rushed to find him in the barn when her chores were done. His face paled and his hands shook as she told him the news; the thought of his father's anger turning his strength to jelly. Mr Williams was a God-fearing man, a devout Methodist who read the Bible to the family at the end of every day, who never missed Sunday service. He would certainly see this as a disgrace. By far the braver of the two, Margaret stood her ground.

'It must be faced Walter. It won't go away. We must tell him this evening after supper.'

She had flounced away and buried herself in work, cleaning and polishing like a woman possessed, baking a huge batch of Welsh cakes to the delight of the children and allowing them some flour and water dough to play with.

As usual, there was little conversation at the meal table; once grace had been said, their long busy days meant that everybody settled to the task of eating rather than talking. Margaret's stew was as tasty as ever, the meat tender and the vegetables soft. But she could barely swallow her small portion and, when she looked across at Walter, he too seemed to be having difficulty in emptying his plate, although Mr Williams would countenance no waste, and eventually the plates were cleared. Margaret left the table and began to prepare Huw and Gwyneth for their beds, taking them upstairs to the room adjoining hers where their truckle beds lay side by side under the eaves. Once the children were settled, she told them their favourite story of Daniel and the lions' den, before blowing out the candle and making her way back down the stairs.

Only Miss Flo was still in the kitchen, washing the china, so Margaret moved quickly, picking up a towel and drying the plates before returning them to their places on the dresser.

'Are you all right, Margaret? You seem quiet today, have you and Walter had a falling out?'

Miss Flo had been aware of the young people's romance and had turned a blind eye to their evening walks and secret smiles. She had no wish to lose Margaret, she valued her hard work, while her lively presence made life bearable, shut away as she was at the end of a long lane, far removed from company and conversation.

'Walter and I need to speak to you and Mr Williams this evening, Miss. I'm not too sure what he will make of our news.'

Something in her face – a tension, a slight twitch at the side of her mouth – showed that Miss Flo knew at once what had happened. Her hand raised to her mouth, and hot soapy water dripped down the front of her dress as she gasped, 'Oh, no, Margaret. Surely not? Couldn't you have waited? This won't go well but I'll do what I can.'

The two women finished the chores, leaving the kitchen

clean and ready for the next day and its round of meals. They removed their aprons and walked slowly through to the parlour. Walter and his father were already sitting, one each side of the fire, Mr Williams engrossed in his newspaper and Walter once again adding neat figures to the farm's account ledger.

Margaret crossed to Walter's chair and stood behind him, nudging him forcefully with her hand.

His face was white and she could feel the fear emanating from him. He coughed and then began, 'Father, Miss Flo, there's something we would like to ask you, Margaret and me. We would like to ask if we could have your permission to wed? We would like to announce our betrothal and have the banns called at chapel.'

'Betrothal? Is this right? Did you know of this Florence? Have you two been plotting behind my back? This is the first I have heard of such a courtship?'

He looked across at his wife, her expression giving away that she did know of the bond between the two young people. Before she could answer he rose to his feet.

'Florence, why did you not tell me? We have a responsibility for Margaret, she is in our employment. Why must the banns be called now? Winter is no time for a wedding. It will be hard for your parents to make the journey, Margaret. I shall allow the two of you to walk out together and we will think again in the spring of calling the banns, when we have all had time to get used to the idea. You must write to your parents, Margaret, and tell them that you are now walking out with Walter.'

'It cannot be the spring, sir,' said Margaret quietly. 'I am expecting a child and it will be born in early summer. Spring will be much too late.'

Rounding on his son, Mr Williams roared with anger.

'Have I not taught you better than this, Walter? Margaret, I took you in and we have treated you as one of the family, fed and clothed you and paid you a good wage for all your hard work. How could you repay me by doing this? Word will get out, you know. People are not stupid, and what will they think at the Big House? This will not reflect well on us at Cefn Barach and I will be a laughing stock in Trefeglwys. I can see it now in the Red Lion – old man Williams can't control that son of his!'

Miss Flo turned as if to speak but he raised his hand to silence her.

'No Florence, I know how fond you are of the girl, but she must leave. There is no other solution. When I go to market next week Margaret, I will take you with me. You must go home to Cancoed, there is no place for you here any longer.'

Chapter 7

IT WAS A difficult homecoming, so different from all the happy occasions of the past few years. She had sat in silence on the journey back to Llanidloes, her small bag of belongings nestled at her feet, her eyes gazing straight ahead.

In the final few days at the farm, she had not spent even a minute alone with Walter. He had busied himself outdoors as much as possible, his head down and shoulders bowed. There had been many tears shed as Margaret realised that she would definitely be leaving. She would miss Huw and Gwyneth, they had always been at her side as she worked in the house and garden, laughing and playing their own special games, as twins so often do. And how would she get through the days without Miss Flo at her side? The two women – thrown together by circumstance – had become real friends. Both had gained in maturity and competence through sharing their respective knowledge, skills and resources. On the one hand, Miss Flo had become a competent mother, cook and housewife. On the other, the access Margaret had been given to a proper library and interesting conversation had broadened her knowledge of the world. Neither woman was looking forward to Margaret's departure, for Miss Flo would undoubtedly be lonely, and Margaret had to face the challenge of telling her news to her parents, and building a new life whilst caring for a child.

From the moment she had stood before her father in the

market square and seen the look of disappointment in his eyes, Margaret had vowed never to apologise for what had happened. She had not been the only person responsible for this child and she was not going to bear the burden of all the guilt. She had sat quietly at the rear of the market stall, saying little and waiting until he had concluded the day's trading. Finally, the stall was clear and the empty boxes and sacks were loaded on to the cart, along with the provisions requested by her mother.

It was only as they climbed through the trees, bare now that the winter winds had cleared away most of their leaves, past the Severn – cascading down on its way to the Shropshire plain and out to the sea – and ascending higher still up the valley and into the rugged hills, that Margaret's tears fell. She turned away from her father, trying to hide her sadness, seeing – as if for the first time – the beauty of the countryside around her while her tears dripped from her cheeks and stained the dark grey wool of her Sunday dress. Touching her hand briefly, her father, Richard Davies, spoke.

'It'll work out, Margaret. Things usually do. Quiet now, and calm yourself before you see your mam.'

The pony and cart turned right into the lane and drew to a halt at the back of the house. Apart from the annual visits home, it had been five years since Margaret had left. She had departed as a girl – afraid of the new life which had been forced upon her – and now she was returning, not only as a woman, but one who was soon to bring another life into the world. And she had no means of providing for the child! She felt overwhelmed by the problems ahead. Her father helped her down and turned her towards the house, 'One day at a time lass, that's how to face it.'

Her mother had been surprised to see her – delighted to have time with her precious eldest daughter – before surprise had given way to curiosity and concern. As the whole sad story had tumbled out, she had taken Margaret into her arms as if she were still six years old, rocking her gently and patting her back in comfort.

'So, it's happened again,' she said, enigmatically. 'Believe me when I say it, Margaret, that I know it's not your fault alone! It can be hard when you have feelings that are hard to check… but for that family to refuse to support you, to throw you out like this? How dare David Williams make a judgement that you are not good enough for his son? At least Richard stood by me and we were wed.'

She had spoken without thinking, her anger getting the better of her usual caution and now she looked at Margaret and saw the realisation in her daughter's face.

'Yes love, me too. It was just the same and for many others as well, but at least most men do the decent thing. But you're home now and things will work out, you'll see. Now go and put your bag in your old room. Ann can sleep down here for a few nights. She's off at the beginning of the week to start work as a maid. There'll be room here for you and your baby.'

*

On a warm May day in 1882, little Edward David Davies took his first breath. Margaret had endured a long and hard labour; she had paced the floor of the small bedroom, back and forth from one wall to the other until the pains had become too severe. With only her mother's help and an old towel tied to the head of the iron bedstead on which to grip, pull or even bite, she had felt her body tighten and ease, over and over again, until she had been certain that it would prove too much and she would die.

Suddenly the pains had altered – her urge to bear down bringing a new focus and determination – and within a matter of minutes she was holding her son. Mother and daughter looked down on the baby with tears of relief and joy. Margaret had not been prepared for the rush of love, the sweeping feelings of devotion and protection that had swamped her. Throughout her pregnancy she had been well, had worked hard, making herself useful inside and out, using physical work as a way to put at a distance her sadness about all that had happened. Apart from sewing tiny clothes and preparing napkins and blankets, she had given little thought to the child she would bear.

Young and strong, Margaret was soon recovered from her labour, and – within the week – was on her feet, not afforded the luxury of lying in for three weeks as privileged ladies did. Edward – or Teddy, as he was soon known – was a happy baby. Between feeds, he would lie in the old wooden cradle, sleeping or gazing at the world around him. After all the heartache and worry, the sadness and shame, suddenly there was laughter and sunshine again at Cancoed, as the little baby grew into a chubby toddler, charming his grandparents and uncles and aunties when they came to visit.

Chapter 8

MARGARET'S DAILY LIFE soon found a pace and rhythm, as she moved between caring for Teddy and attending to chores around the farm, freeing Meg from many of the heavier jobs. With a child of her own she was more aware and understanding of the toll that childbirth and motherhood take, and began to appreciate more fully that her mother had borne six children, one of whom had died only moments after birth. Her mother's dark hair was now turning silver and her face showing lines of tiredness, her hands knotted with arthritis from the hours spent working in the wet and cold.

Wanting to be able to contribute to the family purse, Margaret had succeeded in building up the flock of hens and ducks, and was now supplying eggs to many of the local houses, with regular orders to wealthy families and local shops. Tuesdays and Fridays were her delivery days, and – having filled her baskets – she took young Teddy, and together they walked across the lower fields and over the small bridge crossing the Severn. As usual she had laid down the baskets carefully before dropping sticks into the water with Teddy, then rushing to see whose stick would reappear first on the other side.

'Mine today, Mam, look, look!' Teddy shouted with delight as he watched his stick race down the river, carried by the swirling water, careering between the boulders. After the game, they had continued on their way, calling at the first two houses to leave their brown hens' eggs and at the second house, an additional half-dozen of the large pale blue duck eggs, much loved by George Forrester for his breakfast. Heading down the hill and back towards Glan-y-nant, Margaret paused to chat to two ladies heading to the village shop.

'Are you bringing eggs, Margaret? Mrs Evans has none left inside.'

'Yes, I've plenty. Can you keep an eye on Teddy while I drop them off? Teddy, you stay away from the wood shed, there's dangerous tools and sharp saws in there. You play with Davy and Stan.'

Teddy nodded and smiled at his mother, settling to play with a few small marbles on the ground with the older boys, whilst the women resumed their gossiping.

The accident happened in seconds, although to Margaret it was as if time slowed right down and she watched it all play out in slow motion. Standing in the door of the little shop, poised to step over the threshold, she saw a large ginger dog appear from the back of the wood yard. It made a beeline for the boys, its lip curling back as it snarled, its muscles coiled with tension and aggression, spoiling for a fight. The older two boys, sensing danger, took cover behind their mothers who shouted at the dog, one running towards it flapping her apron in an attempt to frighten it away. Teddy rose to his feet but froze with fear for the dog fast approaching was nothing like Poll, the old sheepdog who followed his *taid* around the farm. Margaret took off at a run but – before she could reach Teddy – the dog had pounced, grabbing him by the leg and shaking his small limb ferociously. Teddy's screams and the shouts of the women brought Bill, the carpenter, running from the wood shed. He aimed a kick at the dog with his heavy work boot, sending it slinking away, yelping in pain. Teddy fell to the floor, whimpering and white with shock and pain as Margaret reached him.

They were soon surrounded by the women and Mrs Evans from the shop, one tearing off a strip of clean white linen from her underskirt for Margaret to cover the jagged bite. Bill took one look at Teddy's pale face and offered to help.

'You'll not walk the young 'un home like that, Margaret. I'll hitch the pony up and take you back in the cart.'

She mumbled her thanks – her eyes never leaving her son – and wondering just how she and her mother would be able to heal the gaping wound in his leg.

Within an hour, they were back in Cancoed; Teddy sitting in silence on the settle with a cup of warm milk, liberally sweetened with honey. His grandmother had taken one look at his leg, pursed her lips, a frown gathering on her forehead as she hurried to gather all she could use to dress the wound. Hot water and salt, cloths and bandages were all used to clean the wound as best she could whilst Margaret held the little boy firmly. As the salty water made contact with his raw flesh, his screams could be heard outside and soon his *taid* was rushing in to see for himself what was happening.

'Whatever is all the noise about?' he cried, stopping in his tracks.

Teddy's cries had increased as soon as he saw Poll loping in beside his grandfather, and he shrank in to his mother's body, shaking with fear. Poll could not understand why he wasn't running to greet her as he normally would and the sharp tone of her master's voice as he ordered her to 'lie down!' sent her slinking under the kitchen table.

With his leg bandaged, Teddy was quiet and, lulled by his grandmother's soft singing, fell asleep in the chair. The adults sat round the table drinking strong sweet tea, a comfort to them all after the shock.

'Whose dog was it? I shall go and speak with the owner. The animal must be put down. I'll take the gun and do it myself.' Richard's voice was quiet but nonetheless determined.

'I don't know, it came from somewhere round the back of the wood shed but it's not Bill's. He said he'd never seen it before. I'll never forget the look on Teddy's face. He was so frightened!'

Her mother refilled their cups and laid her hand gently on the little boy's head.

'We must watch this little one. God knows where that dirty dog had been, what filth he carried. It's not going to be easy Margaret, but we are going to have to bathe that wound three or four times a day to keep it clean as it heals. He's a strong little lad though, he'll be fine.'

Over the next day, her promise would be put to the test. Their cheerful robust Teddy seemed to shrink before their eyes and grow quieter by the hour. He bore their ministrations stoically, making little fuss as they cleaned the wound, but by the second evening, a fever took hold of him and he alternated between sweating and shivering. The area around the wound grew hot and swollen and, as his temperature rose, he refused all offers of drinks.

Margaret knew that they had nowhere near enough money to call out the doctor and she could do little but trust in her mother's healing skills. The wound was covered in a bread poultice to draw out the infection and the two women sat with the little boy throughout the long night, alternately sponging his hot body and then adding blankets when he shook with the force of the fever. But as the skies began to lighten, Teddy's eyes darkened and became fixed on a spot near the dresser, almost as if he could see something or someone in the corner of the room. Minutes later he slumped in his mother's arms, his breathing becoming more and more laboured as his little body fought the infection.

Then he was gone. One minute there, the next not. There was no sudden crisis, no thrashing, no gasping for breath, nothing more than a quiet sigh, an absence and his weight settled more deeply onto his mother.

Chapter 9

MARGARET FELT AS though she was split in two; one part of her watched her mother stroke Teddy's head before getting up to fill the kettle. She could see that her mother wasn't crying but her body was somehow smaller, diminished by what had just happened. The other part of her held tightly to Teddy as if she could never bear to loosen her hold on him. For folk like them death was commonplace, part of life. Children died all the time from influenza, consumption, infections and accidents. There was little you could do if you had no money. No money, no doctor. No doctor, no treatment, but who knew if even the doctor could have saved him.

Meg placed a cup of tea next to Margaret, patted her shoulder and made her way up the narrow staircase to break the news to her husband. Margaret sat with her dead son on her lap, cradling his head and singing softly the hymns she had known since childhood. Her heart felt cold and heavy, her eyes burning with exhaustion and unshed tears.

Within days, the funeral had been arranged; the folk of the Glan-y-nant valley had shown themselves to be true friends and neighbours, for Margaret was popular, largely as a result of her willingness to undertake hard work and her ready smile. Bill, the carpenter, had arrived with a small coffin, refusing any suggestion of payment. The Rev. Matthias had waived the usual fee for delivering a service and committal when he had visited the farm to discuss with Margaret the order of service. Her former Sunday school teacher, Miss Evans, would play the harmonium, so that soon the only requirements remaining were that Margaret should select the hymns to start and end the funeral service. She made her decisions calmly, choosing 'Gwahoddiad' and 'Ar Hyd y Nos', the hymns most loved by the family and known by all the local folk, who could then sing from memory without hymn books.

In the days following Teddy's death, Margaret shed no tears; hers was a stony and cold grief. Her young face was set in the stern lines of a much older woman, one worn down by life's knocks. Her hair was scraped back, pulled tightly into a plait, with no suggestion of an escaping ringlet. She had eaten very little and her tall slender figure was unbending in the confines of her black bombazine dress. This had arrived on a cart, brought across by one of the gardeners from the Fron, a kind gesture from Mrs Lewis, one of her regular egg customers. For this and many other kindnesses, Margaret was grateful but she found it difficult to give more than a nod of thanks to anyone, for fear that she would lose control of her emotions and finally break down. This day had to be survived, somehow.

It was a bright, clear day and the sun shone through the gaps between the leaves and branches, sprinkling the scene with shafts of light. Margaret and her mother left the house together, following her younger sisters Lizzie and Ann who were sitting in the back of the cart with the tiny wooden coffin resting at their feet. Her father was already sitting in the front; holding the reins in one hand, he reached with the other to help her on to the seat beside him. Once she and her mother were settled, the pony moved off, his feet ringing out a mournful beat on the old cobbles. Margaret's brothers

Richard and William walked behind; dressed in their Sunday best, they carried their cloth caps and showed no signs of their usual banter and mischief.

The journey to Cefn Chapel took almost an hour; one in which Margaret focused straight ahead, not daring to turn her head and catch a glimpse of the coffin containing her young son. The doors to the chapel were open, the sound of the organ music reaching their ears as Richard slowed the pony. The building was low and squat, functional in appearance, having little in the way of adornment on its whitewashed walls. Its purpose was clear: a place to house the faithful, to allow the congregation to shelter from the elements whilst they gave praise, a place of sanctuary and solace on a day such as this.

Her father lifted the coffin from the cart and, with bowed head, carried his grandson to the doors of the chapel where the Rev. Matthias stood waiting. It was a simple procession, the reverend followed by the grandfather carrying his grandson, Margaret and her mother with the younger siblings behind them.

The small chapel was full of people, mostly women and children, as it was a working day and few could afford to be away from their jobs. As Miss Evans began to play and the first notes of 'Gwahoddiad' washed over them, the congregation rose to their feet and showed their sorrow and respect in a way that came so naturally. They sang. The little building was filled to overflowing with a blend of voices, an outpouring of feeling which seemed to release the tension that had been holding Margaret together so that, at last, her tears fell.

At the end of the service the chapel door opened, and the congregation returned to the sunshine which seemed unnaturally bright after the darkness of the building. They walked the short distance to the cemetery, the wind sighing and moaning as it moved through the dark crescent of pine trees which gave shelter to the chapel. To Margaret's eyes, it was if the trees were standing guard over the graves, their branches swaying and bending as if to protect the souls in their care.

The family had reached the newly-dug grave, close to those of her grandparents. As the Rev. Matthias' deep voice began to speak the words of the committal, her father stepped forward and lowered the coffin into the ground. Taking the bunch of wild flowers that her mother had gathered that morning, Margaret dropped them onto the coffin; the bright colours of campion, buttercups and cow parsley looking so out of place in the depths of the dark hole.

From some place deep within her, Margaret found the strength to stand with her parents and to shake the hands of those who had come to support her. Her face was taut with tension, her head screaming with bands of pain. At last, they were left alone with just the reverend and Miss Evans. Taking her hands firmly, the white-haired old lady looked directly into her eyes.

'It will get easier, Margaret. You will never forget this little boy but the pain will fade. You are a young woman and there is time for you to have another family. You may not feel like that now, but things can change in time.'

Margaret had always liked Miss Evans. It was she who had taught her Bible stories and hymns, and helped foster her love of reading, but she could not stop the words which poured out. Her dark eyes burned as she turned them on her old teacher.

'I know you mean well Miss Evans, but there will be no man in my life, no more children. I have finished with all that now. Things will have to change and I will have to leave and find work again. I can't be a burden on my parents, and work will be good for me now. That's what I am going to do. I shall work.'

Chapter 10

WINTER HAD BEGUN to take hold in the Severn valley; morning frosts cloaked hedgerows and bushes with a crisp white icing, and the inside of the bedroom windows were opaque with a layer of frost which took all morning to thaw, leaving small puddles on the windowsills and a slow steady drip onto the floorboards beneath. All the chores on the farm became more difficult, the animals needed extra hay carrying to them, ice on water troughs had to be broken, and livestock checked daily as the sheep were now in lamb.

But not even a cold morning and her endless round of repetitive tasks could dampen Margaret's spirits on this November day. She had heard about a job: a post as kitchen maid for Mr Jenkins, the town clerk. Like most menial positions, it hadn't been advertised in the *Montgomeryshire Express*, for most looking for such work could neither read nor afford to buy newspapers. At chapel on the previous Sunday, she had been approached by Mrs Watkins, wife of Jack Watkins, who sat on the town council, along with John Jenkins, and had come home and told his wife that Mr Jenkins' current kitchen maid was leaving to get married and that John was looking for a replacement. Mrs Watkins had immediately thought of Margaret, having overheard her outburst after Teddy's funeral. Penygreen – sitting on the edge of town – was not too far away, but it would give Margaret a chance to leave home, to rebuild her life again.

After two days of thinking incessantly about the possibility, considering all sides of the issue, Margaret had finally thrown off her fears that the house would be too grand and her background too lowly. Today was the day that she would present herself for consideration. She had discussed it with her mother and they had both agreed that it would be pointless to arrive on a morning. Mornings were busy. These were the hours when most chores were completed, rooms cleaned, fires lit, meals cooked and laundry washed. Early afternoon would be the best time.

Having heated some water on the stove, Margaret stripped down to her petticoat in the scullery, and washed as best as she could before loosening her long black hair and brushing it until it shone. The smartest dress she owned was the black bombazine so she took it from the closet, shook out its folds and was instantly back at the graveside, looking for the last time before the soil began to fall on top of Teddy's coffin. Shaking her head at the memories, she stepped into the dress. She had no choice if she wanted to make a good impression. With her hair tied back again, she placed her mother's neat hat on her head and wrapped her Sunday shawl around her shoulders. She would have to do.

It was a good four-mile walk to the outskirts of Llanidloes, to Penygreen. She remembered the house from her trips in and out of town when she had made her visits home from Trefeglwys, but now that she was actually walking up the drive, between white stone pillars either side of the large iron gates, it seemed to have grown. The elegant Georgian proportions of the house, three floors with bowed, leaded windows sitting either side of the grand front door, made her feel very small and insignificant. Compared to Cancoed, this was a mansion, if not a palace.

A small path led from the main drive round to the rear of the house, and she followed this, her instinct telling her that the front door was definitely not for those applying for the position of kitchen maid. The yard at the back of the house was clean and orderly. A wood store and coalhouse, both well stocked, stood next to a brick-built washhouse, and through the open door she could see a large copper standing above a fireplace. Beyond the cobbled yard was a vegetable garden where she could see cabbages and onions still growing. A few bare fruit trees stood at the far end, and at the side of the house was a lawn, surrounded by flowerbeds and crossed by two sturdy washing lines. Her breathing slowed; at least this was all familiar to her and, as for the rest, well, she would think of it like home, only larger. She needed this job, needed to get away from all the painful memories and to prove she could better herself.

Quickly, before she could change her mind and scuttle back down the drive to the safety of her old life, she marched across the cobbles and lifted the heavy knocker on the dark green door. In a few minutes, she heard steps; someone was moving slowly and with an uneven gait. The door opened. Standing framed in the doorway was an old lady, short and stout with small spectacles perched on the end of her nose. She smiled kindly at Margaret.

'Yes, what is it dear? Are you selling something?'

'No, I'm not selling anything. I've come about the kitchen maid job. Mrs Watkins told me you were looking for a kitchen maid.'

The old lady looked Margaret up and down, taking in her good dress, her tidy appearance and polite manner.

'Come in out of the cold dear. Just there, go into the kitchen.'

She pointed to a door on the left and closed the outer door before following Margaret into the largest room she had ever seen. Her days at Tŷ Uchaf had shown her a home larger that her family had, but nothing had prepared her for the size and scale of this kitchen. Within an hour, Margaret found herself back outside the door again, her feet automatically turning for home while her mind whirled with the conversation she had had. The post was hers. She would start the following Monday and would have bed and board and work to do; she would no longer be a drain on her family and she would be busy from morning until night.

*

Penygreen was a quiet house; John Jenkins a quiet man. Not taciturn or morose but thoughtful, pensive, a man who would never use a dozen words when six would suffice. A long-serving member of Montgomeryshire County Council and town clerk in Llanidloes, Jenkins was a devout man, a stalwart member of the Congregational Church, a Liberal and a well-educated and literary man, having written and published essays on law reform, national education and the poetry of Wales. A lifelong bachelor, he asked nothing more of his domestic staff than regular meals: breakfast at eight o'clock, lunch at one, a light supper at six-thirty, fresh laundry and an orderly and clean home.

Margaret had been working as kitchen maid for nearly a

year when she had her first conversation with her employer. He had returned to the house early after a meeting and found Margaret on her knees in the library, rolling newspapers in order to light the fire. This small room at the rear of the house was John Jenkins' favourite place to sit of an evening; here he would read, write and enjoy the comfort of a warm fire and a pipe of tobacco. He rarely used the more imposing parlour unless he was entertaining, and those occasions were becoming far fewer now that he was in his late seventies.

Rising to her feet, Margaret bobbed, in a strange blend of bow and curtsey, feeling unsure what was expected. Until now, her daily routine had been structured so that she could complete her tasks without bothering the owner of the house, and so the two had never before come face to face.

'Good afternoon, Margaret.' He spoke gently and with a smile in his deep-set eyes.

'Carry on, it's quite all right. I am sorry to have startled you. The council meeting was unexpectedly short and I didn't linger down in the town as it is such a cold and miserable day.'

'Thank you, sir. I'll have it alight in just a minute.'

She finished rolling the papers, twisting them into tight knots before laying them neatly on the hearth. Next came a framework of morning sticks and finally – piece by piece – the dark glistening coal. Striking a match, she deftly set fire to the paper at either side of the hearth and then, using the heavy leather bellows, she encouraged the flames to expand. Within a few minutes, the fire took hold and she added some more coal. Getting to her feet, she shook out her coarse brown apron, picked up the bucket which had held papers and sticks, and turned to leave the room. She stopped as John Jenkins spoke again.

'Have you settled in, Margaret? Are you enjoying the work?'

Such a level of interest in her wellbeing was so unusual that Margaret had to stop for a minute and consider her reply.

'Thank you, sir, yes I am. I have learned a great deal already. Mrs Griffiths is a wonderful teacher and I have learned to cook so many new recipes and how to clean all your beautiful things. It has opened my eyes, sir, to so much. And it is so peaceful here, so quiet. I love the quiet.'

Realising that her tongue was running away with her, Margaret quickly brought her chatter to a close. Another smile played on the old gentleman's face and he moved to sit in the leather armchair next to the fireplace.

'I am glad that you are content. Mrs Griffiths tells me that you are a diligent young woman and have eased her burden considerably. She has been a loyal servant to me and I am glad to have her still, but she is almost as ancient as me and I have no desire to overwork her.'

'Thank you, sir. Could I fetch you some tea? You must be chilled after your walk home.'

'That would be lovely, and some of that excellent fruit cake which has been appearing of late, if we have some?'

Margaret smiled. 'That's my mam's recipe, sir. She will be very pleased to know that you like it.'

With that, she scuttled away to the kitchen to prepare the tea tray. As she bustled around collecting china, slicing cake and putting the heavy kettle back on the stove to boil, her thoughts ranged back over the last year.

*

She had passed the anniversary of Teddy's death at Penygreen; that had been an awful day when everything she had attempted had gone wrong. Finally, just before lunch, she had dropped the china soup bowl, sending shards of porcelain and splashes of chicken soup across the kitchen table and quarry-tiled floor before bursting into tears of frustration and grief.

Mrs Griffiths had sat her down, finished serving lunch to Mr Jenkins, before returning to the kitchen and setting down before Margaret a cup of tea. When the tea was drunk and Margaret's tears were coming to an end, she had insisted on knowing what had caused the outburst. Once started, the story had poured out between sniffs and gulps, including the significance of that very date.

Sympathy had shown in every line of Mrs Griffiths' face and she had stood up, patted her gently on the shoulder.

'You poor young lady. Well, this hard day is nearly over and once we have had some soup ourselves, we shall spend the afternoon cleaning all the brass. There's nothing like some polishing to take your mind off your troubles.'

That day, something had changed within the house; such a small change as to almost go unnoticed but there was a new closeness between the two women, and as Margaret learned more about how to care for the fine furniture, beautiful glassware and framed oil paintings, Mrs Griffiths slowly loosened her hold on the reins of the house, allowing Margaret to become more involved and take greater responsibility.

Caring for this impressive house and all its treasures had proved to be a healing experience. Working in its peaceful rooms provided a daily solace for Margaret and, after so many years of sharing first her family home and then Tŷ Uchaf, she responded to the solitude and silence with gratitude. As she became more adept at the daily tasks, she could allow her mind to wander.

It wasn't just Margaret's life that had changed; much was changing in the world around her. Mr Jenkins was a great reader, and the newspapers were delivered every morning in time for his breakfast, now that the mail train came in from Newtown each morning. It was now 1885 and she would see the headlines when she cleared away the breakfast dishes. At the end of the day, the papers would go to the kitchen where they were used for lighting fires and cleaning windows, but first she and Mrs Griffiths would read them together when their day's work was done. Along with deaths and births, wars and elections, they read about the slowly growing movement to give women the vote.

In recent years, a far greater percentage of men had been given the franchise, and this had increased the desire of many women to be able to have the same right. Tucked away in rural mid Wales, there was little outward show of rebellion and dissention but people – women – were talking about the possibility of change. Sitting close to the warmth of the black range, Margaret wondered what difference it would make to her life if she could vote? Would she feel more in control of her future?

For the moment, she was content with her lot. She had her own small room in the attic, simply furnished but with ample bed covers for the cold winter nights, as well as use of a stone hot water bottle which made it so much easier to creep between the sheets at the end of the day. She was paid well for her work, and paid quarterly, so she did not have to wait a full year for any financial reward for her work. Out of her wages, she was able to send some home to Cancoed to repay her parents for all their kindness and support when she and Teddy had lived there with them. She had enough to save a little, and at the end of September she had been able to go to David Jones, the drapers, and buy some new bloomers and a chemise. She was so proud of these garments that she could barely bring herself to wear them, keeping them for Sundays when she went to chapel. Never before had she owned anything which had been bought as new, and she saw this as a measure of her success.

Margaret was not a greedy person but the food served in Penygreen was of good quality, and both she and Mrs Griffiths ate the same meals as their master, so Margaret was now enjoying a diet with plenty of protein and a variety of fruit and vegetables, all of which had allowed her figure to fill out again after the months of grieving. Her hair shone, her skin bloomed and anyone watching her make her way into Llanidloes on her weekly afternoon off work would see a striking young woman, light of step and with a ready smile for those she met along the way. Life at Penygreen had been kind to her.

Chapter 11

MARGARET WOKE TO the sound of rain lashing against her window and a steady drip from the lead drainpipe onto the stone windowsill. She had mentioned to Mr Jenkins that the guttering was broken some months ago but as yet he had done nothing about it. Like many clever and bookish people, his mind was never on the practicalities, and she guessed that she would have to speak to the odd-job man herself and then remind her employer. The weather had made the autumn morning darker than usual, but she knew that it was time she should be up. Over the last year, she had taken over responsibility for all the early morning chores and breakfast preparation, to allow Mrs Griffiths to rise a little later and take her time over her morning routine; the old lady was becoming increasingly troubled with rheumatism and everything took longer to complete than it had a year ago.

After a quick wash in the cold water that she had carried up the stairs the previous evening, Margaret pulled on her warm underclothes, petticoat and grey morning dress and ran down the stairs to the kitchen. Thankful that the fire in the range was still glowing, she riddled the ashes vigorously, causing the dying embers to glow red before piling on more coal. With the air vent open, the fire was soon roaring and she placed the kettle to boil and began the process of making the morning porridge. She smiled as she added the creamy milk to the oats and a pinch of salt, no need to use water here, as she had done so many times in her childhood if the cow had little milk.

Moving in to the dining room, she lit the ready-laid fire, set a place at the table for Mr Jenkins, and went to collect the newspapers from the front hall. Shaking out the *Montgomeryshire Express*, she looked for a moment at the front page. Scanning quickly, she found what she had been looking for. Each week, the paper carried an episode of the book *The Adventures of Caradoc* by Christabel Hardy. These romantic tales of knights and damsels in distress had captivated Margaret's imagination. Today's edition held the fifth instalment, 'How Young Sir Christopher Fought the Good Fight', and she was already looking forward to reading it aloud to Mrs Griffiths after their working day was over. None of the train excursions, fat stock sales or advertisements for lodgings in Aberystwyth was of the slightest interest to her; they could not compete with the tales of adventure which lay in hiding on page eleven. She folded the paper carefully and placed it with the *Western Daily Mail* on the table for Mr Jenkins.

Breakfast was long finished, and Margaret was busy in the kitchen chopping beef and onions in preparation for lunch when a knock sounded on the back door. She wiped her hands and went to open it.

'Morning, Miss Butcher's order from Hamers, can you sign the book, Miss?'

Putting the basket of meat on the table, Margaret realised that Mrs Griffiths was still not down and in the kitchen. It was always the housekeeper who signed for deliveries, but she would have to do it today and explain later.

'Just here, is that right?'

Using the butcher boy's stubby pencil, she carefully signed

her name and closed the door. A look at the wall clock showed her that it was past nine-thirty and well after the usual time that the old lady would be down ready for work. Where was she? Worried that she was unwell, Margaret put the finishing touches to the stew and placed the dish in the oven. As she climbed the staircase, she felt anxious; she had never been across the threshold of the old lady's room, not even to clean, as Mrs Griffiths was adamant that she could clean her own quarters and change her own bed linen. Standing outside the door, she bent her head close to the varnished wood, but there was no sound from the room. She tapped gently, then slightly harder. Still no response.

'Mrs Griffiths, are you all right? Would you like a cup of tea?'

There was no noise at all, no movement. Taking hold of the door handle, Margaret turned the knob and pushed open the door. The room was dimly lit, as the curtains were still drawn but even so she could see that the bed was empty, covers thrown back as if someone had just left its comfort and warmth. She took another step into the room, calling again. 'Mrs Griffiths, are you all right?'

Her eyes had grown accustomed to the half-light, and now she could clearly see a bent and twisted foot at the side of the wardrobe. Moving across, Margaret could see the old lady lying in a crumpled heap, her black dress in her hands. Her face was cold. She pulled back her hand, reaching for the only explanation, which was that Mrs Griffiths had experienced some sort of turn while reaching for her clothes. Margaret knew that she must fetch Mr Jenkins, but it seemed wrong for him to see his housekeeper in this state, with her flannel nightgown pulled under her and displaying her swollen knees and heavily veined legs. She lifted the dress gently from the housekeeper's hands and laid the bedspread across her body, maintaining her respectability and decorum.

Shaking now and feeling quite nauseous, she made the return journey down the stairs, coming to a halt outside the library door. She knocked.

'Come in.'

'Mr Jenkins, sir; I don't know to tell you... but Mrs Griffiths, sir, she hadn't come down, and I've just been up to the room and she's gone. Dead. She's dead, sir.'

At this point, the tears fell and Margaret could no longer contain her distress at finding Mrs Griffiths. This lady had shown her such kindness, taught her so much, and they had shared so many evenings together. What would she do without her?

Mr Jenkins had risen to his feet.

'Show me where she is, come on now.'

Together they made their way to the housekeeper's room. It was the smallest room on the second floor, tucked away at the end of the landing.

'Poor Ellen, she was a loyal friend and servant. We must call for Dr Thomas and I will arrange a funeral service. She had no family Margaret, so you and I, we must be her family. Will you do that with me?'

'Yes, of course, sir. I'm sorry for crying, it was the shock, and she had become my friend. It is so sad.'

'Sad for us who have lost her Margaret, but perhaps not so sad for her. No lingering illness, no real suffering, and she died here in the place she called home whilst she could still carry out some of her duties. She would have hated to feel that she had become a burden. We must be grateful for that. Now, do you think you can manage for the next week or so? We will arrange Mrs Griffiths' funeral, and when it is over we will talk again of how best to organise things in the house.'

'That will be good sir, but for the moment I can do everything.' It was then that she remembered the butcher boy's visit.

'Oh, sir, I had to sign for the meat this morning. That's what made me realise that Mrs Griffiths hadn't come down. I didn't know what else to do, sir.'

'That was the sensible thing to do, Margaret. I will speak with the stores and let them know that you have my permission to place orders and sign for goods. For now, let's try and carry on as normal. I'm sure that's the best thing to do. I shall send Dick with a note for Dr Thomas and you must continue with preparation for lunch. We still need to eat.'

Throughout the day, she had kept busy completing all the chores she would normally have shared with Mrs Griffiths. It wasn't until the last dish had been put away and she had sat in her usual chair to pick up the morning's paper that the realisation of what had happened fully dawned on her. What would happen now? Mr Jenkins would need a new housekeeper. Who would it be? What if she didn't take to Margaret? There would be change again, just as she had begun to settle in to this new life. There was little she could do to alter things, however, so she opened the paper and turned the pages to find the long-awaited instalment of Caradoc, letting the story wash over her and leave no room for her worries.

Chapter 12

AFTER A THIRD wearing, the black bombazine dress had gone back into the cupboard. Having placed it on a wooden hanger, Margaret had put on her day dress and apron and returned to the kitchen to prepare a tea tray for Mr Jenkins. The funeral had been an understated affair, with only a handful of mourners, many of whom belonged to the group of elderly ladies who regularly attended all local funerals in the hope of a plentiful tea afterwards. They had been disappointed on this occasion, as Mr Jenkins had seen no need to supply ham sandwiches and fruit cake to people who had not been friendly to Ellen Griffiths when she had been living and working amongst them. Over the years, there had been rumour and speculation about the reserved gentleman and his housekeeper, all of which had made Ellen wary of female friendship and added fuel to the fire of local gossips. Only John and Ellen knew the truth of their relationship; it had been one of friendship and respect, for Ellen Griffiths had possessed a quick mind and enjoyed a debate on the issues of the day. She had brought a woman's viewpoint to their discussions and helped to convince John Jenkins to support those Liberals who were in favour of votes for women. He had learned much from her and appreciated her restrained ways and thoughtful manner. He had been delighted to learn that Margaret could read when she had joined the household, and he had often heard the two women discussing the latest events, both local and national, as they worked alongside each other. Over the past week, he had given much thought to the future, and today he intended to share those plans with Margaret. He heard the rattle of china on the tray and got up to open the door.

'Thank you, sir.' She placed the tray on the small side table and bent to pour out the tea.

'Leave it for a moment Margaret, I need to speak with you about the future.'

She had known that this conversation would arise and had been dreading it. Clasping her hands firmly behind her back so that their shaking would be hidden, she faced her employer.

'I know, sir. You will be needing a new housekeeper. I have tried this week to carry on just as Mrs Griffiths would have done, sir.'

'I know, Margaret. Why don't you sit down for a moment. Take that seat.'

He indicated a high-backed wooden chair and, uneasily, she sat. He returned to his own chair and sat again.

'I would like to offer you the position of my housekeeper, and then hire a new kitchen maid for you to train up.'

'Me? Be the housekeeper? I never dreamed of that, sir. I am just the kitchen maid.'

'You are far more able than you realise, Margaret. I know how much you have been covering for Mrs Griffiths during these last few months. You know exactly how I like the house to be run. You can read and write and are capable of placing orders and keeping records of all that has been spent. You can present them to me at the end of each month so that I can check that you are managing. How does that sound?'

'Thank you, sir. Thank you for giving me the opportunity.'

Margaret spoke calmly as usual but inside she was bursting with a mix of excitement, pride and fear. A housekeeper? This was her chance to make something of herself, to gain experience and lift herself from the depths to which she had fallen after losing Teddy.

'I'll do my very best, sir. I'll not let you down, and I'll soon get a new girl trained up in the kitchen.'

'I know you will, Margaret. I have every faith in you. I shall ask around and see if we can find a suitable girl. As housekeeper, you will have much more responsibility and I shall double your wages to five guineas a year, with effect from today. I will also make arrangements with Jones' Drapers for you to go and purchase two new dark dresses, and to Edward Rees the shoemaker, where you must choose a new pair of black shoes and a pair of stout boots for the winter weather. These will all be put on my accounts. Depending on the stature of the new kitchen maid, perhaps you will be able to pass on your present uniform dresses? A few alterations may suffice?'

'Thank you sir, I'm sure I shall be able to do that. It's very generous of you, Mr Jenkins. I really don't know how to thank you.'

'You can thank me just by continuing to do your usual good work and allowing things to continue as normal here at Penygreen. Oh, one last thing Margaret, before I let you go and I can enjoy my tea: I would like you to give Mrs Griffiths' room a good clean, send her clothes to the workhouse, for there are many who could make use of them, and let me know if there is a need to replace anything, curtains, rugs and so forth. Once that is done, the room will be yours and you can move your belongings into it, freeing up your attic room for the new maid.'

Unable to sit still for even a minute longer, Margaret rose to her feet, the smile she had tried so hard to contain spreading across her face like sunshine from behind grey clouds.

'Thank you, again! This has been such a strange day; I felt so sad this morning about losing Mrs Griffiths and it was dreadful that she had few friends and no family at her service. I will never forget our voices disappearing up to the ceiling in such a large chapel, but now I feel such joy. I am so grateful for this chance, sir. I will work so hard, and your home will never have a speck of dirt in it. It was a lucky day for me, sir, when Mrs Griffiths took me on as kitchen maid. I won't let you down.'

John Jenkins smiled and waved her to the door.

'Best get to the kitchen then, or supper time will be here. The next few weeks will be busy for you, so make sure that you take your afternoon and evening off and get away room the chores. I see in the paper that there are to be Penny Readings in the Public Rooms this Wednesday. It will be good for you to get out and about and meet more young people.'

'I will, sir, if you are sure I can go. I have always wanted to go but wasn't sure if working girls like me were welcome there.'

'You will find plenty of working girls there Margaret, many from the mills and factories will be sitting in the penny seats. You go once you have served my supper and I will leave my tray in the kitchen for you to see to the next morning. We must all have breaks from our work; it is the breaks that bring us back refreshed to our labours.'

And so, the following Wednesday, with all her chores completed, Margaret washed her face, tidied her hair and put on her hat, wrapped her best shawl around her shoulders and, taking a last look at herself in the mirror, closed the door on her new room. She felt a tingle of apprehension as she made her way downstairs and let herself out of the rear door, taking care to lock it and hide the key under the upturned flowerpot. This was to be her first visit to the Penny Readings and although she had seen the programme on a poster, she was still not quite sure what to expect from the evening.

Clearly, she was not going to be alone, as many people were making their way up Great Oak Street towards the Public Rooms. She had never been into the building before, and was eager to see the interior. She joined the queue all waiting to pay their entrance fee, and was surprised to see a good number of young women like herself. A few were alone, and some stood with friends, but they all seemed to be quite at home amongst the more expensively dressed ladies and gentlemen. Suddenly there was a rush, as the side door opened and all those holding a first- or second-class ticket were allowed to enter. Margaret stood with the remainder waiting to pay their penny fee, and the line inched forward slowly until she found herself at the front and her money had been taken, replaced with a small buff coloured ticket, and she was through the door and crossing the black-and-white tiled entrance and into the hall itself.

Those with tickets were already settled into their seats, clutching programmes and looking around to see who else was in attendance and perhaps, more importantly, to be seen. Llanidloes may only have been a small market town but it had its fair share of inspirational people; the prominent trades people, the owners of mills, mines and flannel factories all had wives who liked to be seen in all the right places. A new outfit could only be truly enjoyed if it was seen and commented on by others, so for them this mutual observation was as an important part of the evening as the music and words which were to follow. For her part, Margaret made her way to a space near the rear of the hall and settled herself next to three young women. The one nearest to her smiled and said, 'Good Evening', before turning her attention back to her companions.

Margaret was content to look around her, taking in the splendour of her surroundings. She had not expected the building to be so large, but it would hold easily as many people as the Congregational chapel. The seats were arranged in curved rows, those at the front being padded, whilst the penny seats at the back were plain wooden benches. She didn't mind in the slightest, for she was there, a part of the evening, and eager now for the performance to begin.

A little over two hours later, Margaret walked from the hall in a daze, her mind whirling from the selection of music and words she had heard. The cocktail of piano playing, recitation, singing and Shakespearean extracts had transported her to an unimagined world. Never had she believed that two hours could pass at such speed. She had been enthralled from the first note of the piano solo to the last line of 'God Save the Queen' and, as she stood waiting for her turn to leave, her neighbour from the penny bench turned to her.

'Your first time then?'

Margaret turned and looked at the young woman. She was short and slightly plump, with a shock of dark curly hair pushed haphazardly under her bonnet as if she had been in a great rush to get ready. Her green eyes smiled and her nose and cheeks were splattered with freckles, giving her an open, honest and trustworthy appearance. Margaret smiled back, breaking free of her trance.

'Yes, my first time but definitely not my last. It was wonderful! Have you been before?'

'Yes. Me and my sister come most weeks if we've been paid on time. We work at Spring Mills, we're spinners. Are you in one of the mills?'

How proud Margaret felt as she gave her answer.

'No, I'm housekeeper to a local gentleman on Penygreen. He suggested I come this evening and I've so enjoyed it. Will there be another next week?'

'Usually. The posters go up on a Saturday, so keep a look out if you're in town. I'll keep an eye out for you next week; I'm Rhiannon.'

'I'm Margaret, Margaret Davies.'

The two women shook hands briefly and then went their separate ways, Margaret's feet seeming to float down Great Oak Street, along Short Bridge Street not noticing the people walking home from the evening or the few staggering home from one of the many public houses. What a week it had been; the sadness of Mrs Griffiths' death had given way to excitement at her promotion, a new room, new dresses now on order, this experience of words and literature, and just possibly a new friend. For the first time in many months, Margaret allowed a flame of hope to burn, a belief that life may yet have much to offer after the sadness of the last few years.

Chapter 13

SOME MONTHS HAD passed. The trees were beginning to shed their leaves, the days were shortening. Life at Penygreen had resumed its rhythm of regular meals, and the week's tasks were once again completed on their allotted day: laundry on Monday, bedrooms cleaned and polished on Tuesday, baking and ironing on Wednesday, a thorough clean of the downstairs rooms on Thursday, glassware, silverware and windows cleaned on Friday, food orders placed on a Saturday and all preparations for the Sunday dinner completed, to leave Sunday as free of work as could be managed. John Jenkins was a firm believer that Sunday was the Lord's Day and not for heavy work; rather, a day of rest, prayer and contemplation.

Working alongside Margaret now was the new kitchen maid, Eliza. A farmer's daughter from Llangurig, she was strong and capable and had settled in quickly, soon learning what was expected of her. Unlike the rest of the household, she was illiterate, and John Jenkins had suggested to Margaret that in the evenings she might like to spend some time teaching Eliza her letters.

Margaret had thought back to her school days, to the time she had spent in the little chapel school at Glan-y-nant, and had begun patiently to help Eliza master the mysteries of the alphabet. Eliza had proved herself to be an able pupil and, after only a few weeks, she was able to read short words and write her own name. It appeared that Margaret had an aptitude for teaching. As the winter of 1887 approached, life for Margaret was full and happy; the days were ordered from the minute she rose from her bed at the sound of the hall clock chiming six, until the moment she returned to her room around nine each evening, eager to get under her covers and lose herself again in the pages of her latest book. Now that she was a resident of the town, she had joined the small public library attached to the Working Men's Institute and was rapidly working her way through their selection of books, happy to read in Welsh or English.

Margaret and Rhiannon had become good friends, meeting every Wednesday evening outside the doors to the Public Rooms, where they would sit side by side and enjoy the evening's entertainment.

One evening, Margaret pulled up the collar of her coat against the dank November evening, linking her arm through Rhiannon's for extra warmth.

'What did you like the best tonight, then?' she asked.

Rhiannon's cheeks creased into a smile.

'That tenor, but not just his voice, mind. Wasn't he handsome, we could do with him to walk us home and keep us warm. What do you think?'

Although she felt a little shocked at her friend's forthrightness, she couldn't help but agree. The man had stood tall and straight, easily over six feet, with broad shoulders, a handsome face and a voice to melt the heart of any woman.

'Come on now, stop your daydreaming, he's not going to be looking at the likes of us. I could see the way he was looking at that soprano in her fine dress. I don't think we stand a chance.'

'Spoilsport, a girl has to dream.'

As they reached the corner of the street where they parted ways before Margaret crossed the river, Rhiannon asked, 'Are you free on Sunday? Shall we walk in the afternoon, if it doesn't rain too much? I'll meet you here at 2.30?'

With that, she scuttled off down the side street, through the rabbit warren of small dark cottages until she reached home: two shared rooms where she and her sister lived above an old couple.

As Margaret walked the final half-mile down the road, she thought – not for the first time – how privileged she was; she may be in service, but she was well fed and clothed and had a warm place to live in. Not for her a shared mattress in an attic room of one of the weavers' houses, with no home comforts or privacy.

She grew to enjoy the time that she and Rhiannon spent together, and the Sunday afternoon walks saw them talk about many subjects. Initially, Margaret was quiet, making only 'yes' or 'no' answers to Rhiannon's ramblings. But over the weeks she became far more confident, and was now an equal participant in their conversations. John Jenkins, a staunch member of the Liberal Party, made no secret of his support for those who were behind the Votes for Women campaign, and both he and Rhiannon were making strong impressions on Margaret. She was now beginning to think that this important change was something worth fighting for. She knew that she had been fortunate in finding her current position, and was determined to make the most of her opportunity by working hard and saving a little money each quarter. The feeling of independence she gained by watching her nest egg grow – the coins hidden away at the bottom of her sewing tin – was precious, and she could completely understand that all women would want to have the same chances.

*

There was high colour in Margaret's cheeks and a swiftness to her walk as she set off one Saturday morning to meet Rhiannon. Mr Jenkins had given his permission for her to leave at eleven in the morning, instead of the usual two o'clock, and she walked smartly across the bridge into town, past the market hall and up Great Oak Street before bearing left, arriving in front of the railway station. Margaret had never been on a train before as she'd had no need to travel far. Today, she and Rhiannon were taking the train to Newtown, where there was to be a public meeting of the newly formed Women's Liberation Federation and a speech by Sybil Thomas on the importance of equality for women workers.

As she walked towards the large main doors, she saw Rhiannon waiting for her by the wall, looking for once a little overawed by her surroundings, and possibly by the thought of the day ahead.

'Hello, Rhiannon, here!'

'I'm glad to see you, I hadn't expected it to be so busy. Come on, let's go and buy our tickets and then we can wait on the platform. I do feel nervous, do you?'

The two women entered the station, queued for their third-class tickets and went to stand on the platform. There were many other people waiting for the train due to arrive in ten minutes' time, and so they moved to the rear of the crowd, not quite sure of what would happen.

They were startled out of their short wait by a loud roar

and clouds of steam appearing. Both women shrank back against the wall. Not even their wildest imaginings could have conjured such a powerful creature, for it really seemed to them both a living thing, snorting and throbbing like some gigantic wild animal. Without conscious thought, they held hands and followed the other passengers, stepping cautiously up in to the rear, third-class carriage and settling themselves on the wooden bench seats. In a matter of minutes, the train gave a lurch, and then the mighty engine began to move them out of the safety of the station. A high-pitched whistle was accompanied by belching clouds of steam, and the train gathered speed until it seemed to Margaret and Rhiannon that they were flying through the countryside. Neither of them had ever experienced such a sense of motion, and their fear gave way to wonder and then giddy excitement as they watched trees, bushes, livestock and cottages flicker past the windows. It was exhilarating, the slight edge of fear and uncertainty only adding to their heightened emotions.

By the time the train slowed and pulled into Newtown station, they were intoxicated with their new experience and in a state of high expectation for what the rest of the day would bring.

Once they arrived at the market hall, joining a crowd of some three hundred people, Sybil Thomas walked on to a raised platform and addressed them. Margaret had read about her in the newspapers and was astounded that such a prominent lady was to be speaking in Newtown. Alongside Margaret and Rhiannon were mostly other women but there was a scattering of men, some members of the Liberal Party and a reporter from the *Montgomeryshire Express*. Sybil Thomas had spoken of the hardships endured by the women of south

Wales, those working in mines, mills and factories. There were accounts of low pay and poor conditions, both at work and in the houses which were rented from the mine and mill owners. There was little provision for children to receive an adequate education, no health care, and life expectancy was low. She ended her talk by rallying to the cause of votes for women because, in her view, until that came about their needs would never be considered or even addressed by legislators and opinion-formers.

Margaret was surprised by the fervour she saw on the faces around her. She had not imagined that there would be so many women thinking as she and Rhiannon did, so many who felt powerless and disillusioned. It was clear from the way that the crowd was dressed that most of them belonged to the working classes. These were women who worked as hard as their menfolk, cared for children and then came home and fed the family, creating homes in dreadful circumstances. These were angry women, women brought to the edge by their feelings of frustration and resentment, by exhaustion and neglect. Women who knew exactly how hard the years ahead of them would be.

Sybil Thomas spoke of herself as a Suffrag*ist* and not a Suffrag*ette*; she spoke of caution when considering their campaign. She urged them always to err on the side of safety, to take a peaceful and non-aggressive stance when putting their views across. Hers was a battle that would be fought with words and not actions. Margaret could see the sense in this but Rhiannon turned to her as they left the meeting with her cheeks burning and eyes flashing with indignation,

'Men will never willingly let us be equal. There will be

no change unless we make it happen. We need to act, to do things, not just talk.'

'But surely, if we break the law it will only make things worse? Some of these women are mothers and they can't afford to be fined or locked up for weeks. There must be a way to make the men, and especially the men with power, listen and understand.'

And so they debated, throwing the argument between them like an old rag doll until finally they reached the point of agreeing to differ: they both felt that change must happen, it was the way that change should be implemented that divided them. Their friendship had become too important to risk and so they agreed to say no more for the moment.

Changing the subject Margaret said, 'I'm so hungry. We've had no time for dinner. Let's see if we can find a little tea room.'

Turning out of the main street, they soon noticed a small black-and-white timbered house with a sign swinging outside. The door opened with the tinkle of a bell and they walked into a room filled with small tables and chairs, each table covered with a brilliant white cloth. The windows were small and leaded, and the room was quite dark so it took a few minutes for their eyes to adjust to the gloom. Standing at the rear was an elderly lady who smiled at them, indicated a table in the centre of the room and asked, 'Tea, ladies? I can do you a pot of tea, bread and butter and a slice of cake for twopence each.'

Margaret's mouth began to water at the thought of food, and her stomach gave a gurgle of protest.

'Yes please. Is that all right, Rhiannon?' At the nod from her friend she repeated, 'Yes please. For both of us.'

It was indeed a day of new experiences, for neither woman

had ever eaten in a public place before. In Llanidloes, there was only one tea room, which was frequented by the wives of the town's traders. Margaret and Rhiannon would not have felt comfortable in there. Besides which, in their own locality there was no need to eat anywhere but in your home; why would you pay for the privilege when you could eat at home? Now, though, as they drank the hot sweet tea and ate the fresh bread, liberally spread with butter and followed with the crumbly fruit cake, they felt as if they had stepped across an important line. They had made their first train journey, attended their first public meeting and were now taking tea in a tea room, and all experiences accomplished without the help of a man.

With an hour to fill before their return train was due, and feeling revived after their simple meal, Rhiannon suggested that they visit the Royal Welsh Warehouse, the famous store owned by Pryce Jones. His business had expanded over the last few years and his mail order company shipped orders of Welsh flannel across Britain and Europe. Rumour had it that even Queen Victoria purchased her flannel drawers from Pryce Jones and was so delighted with them that she had given him a knighthood.

They made their way to the imposing red-brick building, gazing up at the height and grandeur in amazement. Rhiannon pushed the large revolving door, and they moved forwards together and entered a world that was new and startling to them both.

Margaret caught hold of her friend's sleeve, tugging the worn wool so hard that she was in danger of ripping it.

'It's so big! How can all this be for shopping? Look at the cupboards, every drawer is stuffed full. I didn't know there could be so many undergarments in one place! What must it feel like to shop here?'

Pointing to a tall, well-dressed woman with a maid standing at her side, Rhiannon whispered, 'Look at her, over there with the big brown hat. She must be buying for her children, just look at the pile that maid is holding. She's got pants and vests, liberty bodices, woolly stockings; those children will never know what a chilblain feels like.'

Even late on a Saturday afternoon, the shop was busy with customers. The walls were lined from floor to ceiling with wooden drawers, all labelled with their contents: children's underwear, men's long sleeved combinations, ladies woollen stockings and many, many more. Smartly dressed ladies and gentlemen stood behind the wooden counters, serving customers quickly and efficiently, taking their purchases and wrapping them in brown paper and string, as no one would wish to be seen walking from the store with their undergarments on view. Once a receipt had been issued, a duplicate was placed in one of the brass cups suspended above the counters on wires; it would then race along the wire to the cashier's office where the customer would queue to pay for their goods.

The ground floor of this emporium was a hive of activity and noise; the tinkling of the cashier's till, the chatter in both Welsh and English, the opening and closing of drawers and cupboards, the rustle of brown paper all blended into a cacophony that transfixed Margaret. Never had she been in such a shop, had her senses assailed by such busyness, all in one space and continuing with a smooth ebb and flow as satisfied customers left, only to be replaced by new and eager ones. The only comparisons she could make were to that of harvest when all the family worked together in the fields, or attending chapel, when everyone came together to worship. Those occasions, however, were different, because everyone involved was concentrating on a common purpose and so the sounds were rhythmic and in harmony. This was a din.

Rhiannon had been watching her friend's face and started to laugh,

'Too noisy for you? You and your quiet life in the big house, you should visit the factory. If you think this is loud, the noise in the mill is a hundred times worse. You can't hear anyone speak, we all learn to lip read and when you come out at the end of the day it takes a few hours before you can hear properly again. Most of the older workers are deaf!'

Roused from her trance, Margaret looked around her.

'I don't know how you stand it, then. Do you want to buy anything in here?'

'No. I've no money left today. I just wanted to take a look. Makes you think, doesn't it? On the floor above us, all those pairs of flannel bloomers are being packed up and then off they go on the trains to who knows where. All these people walking around dressed in the wool from our sheep, from our hills. I look at sheep quite differently now I work in a mill. If there were no farms and sheep, there'd be no wool, no wool and no mills, no mills and no job for me. I can't say it's a wonderful job but it is work and it's better than being on the streets or married off to some miserable old man just to get a roof over my head. I shall never take sheep for granted again.'

'Me neither. Now let's catch the train and get home to Llanidloes. We've had quite enough excitement for one day.'

They made their way from the shop, strolled back to the station and boarded the train for Llanidloes. The motion of the carriages lulled Margaret into a half-asleep state and her mind roamed over the day's events, leaving her feeling very blessed for all that she had. The Reverend Silin Jones was always telling them to count their blessings, and the day's outing had made her very thankful indeed for her simple life.

Chapter 14

No MATTER HOW content or unhappy we may be, the only thing certain in life is that change will happen. The old century was nearing its end, and life was changing more quickly than ever before as the Industrial Revolution shaped life for the working folk, both in towns and the countryside. Even in the quiet streets of Llanidloes, there was an undercurrent of things just waiting to happen.

Margaret and Rhiannon's shared love of the Penny Reading evenings, and their long discussions on the lives of women, had brought them ever closer. But Rhiannon had been growing increasingly worried about her position at the mill as very many mill owners were laying off workers, and already one of the largest mills had closed its doors. Spring Mills, where she worked, was still producing flannel, but orders were down due to heavy competition from the mills of Lancashire and Yorkshire, where steam-driven engines had increased efficiency and lowered prices. Rhiannon's parents had died many years ago and she and her sister needed reliable work and income to support themselves. It was with regret that they decided to leave Wales and head north to find work in the mills there.

'I shall miss you so much, you and your talking. Who will I find now to debate with? Who will keep me on my toes and point out the best-looking men on a Wednesday evening?' Margaret told her friend.

Margaret tried so hard to stay cheerful but the sight of Rhiannon standing with her sister, along with all their belongings tied into bundles, proved too much and her tears fell, dripping onto the front of her dark coat.

'Come here, cariad!' Rhiannon held her close just as the train pulled in to the station. Then she was collecting up her luggage, running for the train with a wave of her hand and the last Margaret saw was her round smiling face as the engine lumbered out, gaining speed and heading north.

As Margaret walked home the thoughts of the first train journey they had taken together brought tears to her eyes. It would be hard – if not impossible – to find another friend like Rhiannon. Her world had been a different one to Margaret's, but Rhiannon had shared her experiences of working in the mills, her views on the poor treatment of the workers and their families, and opened Margaret's eyes to the full extent of their low pay and poor conditions. She had learned a lot from her friend; she only hoped she had been able to broaden her friend's knowledge in the same way.

Giving herself a mental shake, she picked up speed and walked back to the house, ready to return to her chores. One thing she had learned from old Mrs Griffiths was that keeping busy stopped you dwelling on the sad side of life. As she entered through the back door, she could hear Eliza singing in her usual slightly off-key way. Margaret took down her apron, tied it firmly around her waist and went through to the parlour. Eliza was polishing the big old bureau with vigorous actions, her face glowing from her efforts.

'Steady on Eliza, you'll polish right through the wood if you keep that up!'

The young girl stopped, rose to her feet and looked at the piece of furniture. It was gleaming from her hard work.

'Has she gone then? I'm sure she'll write to you when she gets settled.'

'Yes, the train was on time and you may well be right about the letters, but I will miss her.'

Looking around the room, Margaret smiled with satisfaction as she looked at the polished furniture, beaten rugs and sparkling windows.

'You've done a great job, Eliza. Well done! I think we've time for a cup of tea before preparing Mr Jenkins' supper.'

'Thank you. Just before we go, could you help me to move this bureau? I can't move it on my own and I'm sure the back could do with a brush, at the very least.'

Smiling to herself, Margaret moved towards the bureau and took hold of one end, nodding at Eliza to take the other. 'One, two, three, lift.'

The look on Eliza's face was worth the effort in lifting the heavy oak bureau. She gasped in amazement when she saw that the bureau had no back, nor any real drawers that could be opened. All that was there was a hollow space.

'Your face is a picture! Don't worry, I did the same with Mrs Griffiths who was housekeeper here when I first arrived. It's not really a bureau at all; it's a hiding place for preachers. Mr Jenkins' family were part of the first Congregational worshippers here in Llanidloes, and in those days they had no chapels, so they used to meet in people's houses to have their services. It was a crime for more than five people to meet together to pray, and if the group heard that the magistrates had been spying and that there could be a chance that the minister would be arrested, they hid him in the back of the bureau and pushed it against the wall. The bureau is over two hundred years old now, so every time you polish it in future you can think of all the people who have hidden away inside it.'

Muttering exclamations of amazement, Eliza helped to return the bureau to its position by the wall, and they made their way back to the comfort of the kitchen and the promise of a pot of tea.

*

Woken abruptly in the middle of the night, Margaret sat up and listened carefully. What had she heard? The sound came from downstairs, a rattling of metal followed by mumbling, and John Jenkins' voice rising in confusion and frustration. This was the third time in as many weeks that her sleep had been disturbed in this way. Reaching for the matches, she lit her candle, pulled a shawl around her shoulders and made her way quietly down the stairs. At the end of the hall John Jenkins stood shaking the door handle, doing his best to open it, seemingly unaware that it was still locked and bolted. He was dressed in his nightshirt, his outdoor boots and favourite black hat. The first time that this had happened, Margaret had imagined that he might be sleepwalking, but combined with other strange and unexpected behaviours he was exhibiting during the day, she now realised that he was in fact suffering from some kind of mental senility.

She spoke gently to him. 'Mr Jenkins, sir, it's the middle of the night, not time to go out at all.'

'No, Margaret, I must get to my meeting. The council will be waiting for me.'

'No, sir, not at this time, you are up too early. The meeting will be tomorrow.'

She had recognised after the first occasion that there was little to be gained from fully disagreeing with him; better by far to coax him back up the stairs and to his bed. Usually, by morning, he had forgotten the incident completely and she would return the keys to their rightful place in the lock before he arrived downstairs for his breakfast. On the first night that she had heard him up and about, he had actually opened the front door and was ready to leave the house, so every evening since she had taken the keys and hidden them in the glove drawer of the coat-stand in the hall. She would never have forgiven herself if he had wandered off and some harm had come to him.

Having made sure that he was safely back in bed, his boots and hat removed, she returned to her own room, leaving the door ajar in case he should stir again. The clock chimed four and she knew that she wouldn't be able to sleep any more; there were too many thoughts careering around inside her head. There was no escaping the fact that Mr Jenkins' behaviour was becoming increasingly eccentric. Although he had resigned from his role on the council some years ago, he still worked in the library each morning, writing essays and pieces for the organisations and societies that he supported. Of late, however, his papers were strewn around the room with no order or care; they were left on chairs and tables, even on the floor. Piles of books were now being scattered around the house instead of being returned to their places on the shelves, and only the day before she had found two leather-bound volumes in the coal scuttle. He had also taken to appearing in the kitchen mid-afternoon to demand his lunch, when only two hours previously she would have served him a roast dinner or meat pie, always followed by one of his favourite milk puddings. She knew that she must speak to his nephew, John Davies, when he next paid a visit. There was a hard lump sitting on her chest, the knowledge that this conversation could only create more change in her life, but she was duty-bound to do all she could to support the old man who had been so kind to her at a time when she needed it most.

Only a week later, she opened the door to John Davies, a kindly man in his late forties, with the same bookish air as his uncle.

'Good morning, sir, you'll find Mr Jenkins in the library as usual. Will you be staying for lunch, sir? There's a steak and kidney pie in the oven.'

'Good morning, Margaret. Well, I hadn't been intending to stay long but if it's one of your pies I may have to change my mind. I think I can smell it already, so yes, I will stay and eat with my uncle.'

He began to walk towards the library door as she placed his hat and coat on the stand and Margaret knew that she should seize this moment.

'Excuse me, sir, I wonder if you could spare a moment first. I am concerned about Mr Jenkins and I must tell you what is going on.'

After a conversation in lowered tones, Margaret felt relieved to hear that John Davies had also been getting worried. He, too, had noticed signs of forgetfulness and absent-minded behaviour quite unlike his uncle's usual ways. Margaret's news only served to increase his anxiety.

'Thank you, Margaret, for telling me this. The family will have to step up and take control of the situation. We cannot expect you to shoulder this responsibility alone. Uncle is an old man now and – as his only relation – I will give the matter due consideration. Whatever the outcome, you will be well looked after. We know how well you have cared for him over these last few years.

'Now, you had better go and check on that pie. Don't worry Margaret, we will find a way to deal with the situation.'

Chapter 15

O N THE FIRST of July 1891, Margaret closed the door behind her at Penygreen for the final time. John Jenkins' condition had deteriorated rapidly over the last couple of months and his nephew John, along with his wife, had taken up residence in the house along with their maid and cook/housekeeper. The house would belong to him after his uncle's death, so that had seemed to be the most sensible solution. Eliza had found work with a nearby family and, although they had promised Margaret a roof over her head for as long as she needed, it had only been a matter of weeks before John's wife, Mrs Davies, had mentioned to her that there were many new positions available at Gregynog Hall. The owners, Lord and Lady Sudeley, were planning a summer of festivities and celebrations to mark the twenty-first birthday of their son, Charles. Margaret had seen the advertisement in the *Montgomeryshire Express* and so decided to attend the selection and hiring meeting to be held at the Bear in Newtown.

She had dressed in her smartest clothes and – armed with glowing references from John Davies – she had stood patiently in line with the other women and men who were being considered for work. When it was her turn to enter, she had taken a deep breath, held her head high and walked in and up to the large table. Sitting behind the table was a well-dressed gentleman with neatly combed hair and a dark moustache.

He introduced himself as Mr Scott Owen, Estate Manager, and the lady next to him, pale faced and with greying hair and small spectacles perched on her nose, was Mrs Harris, the housekeeper.

The advertisement had listed many posts: cook, housemaids, valet, gardeners and carpenters, and Margaret had imagined that she may have enough experience to be considered as a housemaid. However, under the encouraging questions from her interviewers, she gave a good account of herself, and when they realised that she was able to read and write and had been solely responsible for the household accounts at Penygreen, a look had passed between them.

Mr Scott Owen spoke, 'Well Miss Davies, we are looking for a cook at Gregynog. Not the senior cook, but someone capable of cooking for the servants' hall and helping Mrs Edwards, our current cook. There are to be many guests staying at Gregynog during the summer and a large amount of catering will be required for Master Charles' birthday celebrations. Do you think you would be happy to take on such a role? It will be hard work and at times very long hours.'

'Yes, sir, I hadn't come expecting such a post but I would be happy to do it. I'm not afraid of hard work.'

Mr Scott Owen had smiled, looked across at Mrs Harris and then spoken again.

'This would be a live-in position; you would have your own room in the servants' quarters with a half-day off each week and one weekend each quarter. The wages would be five guineas a year.'

Shocked by how quickly the interview had passed and what had been suggested, she was incapable of doing more than mumble her acceptance before being handed a slip of paper showing her starting date and instructions for her arrival in Newtown.

So, the first day of July had seen her say her last goodbye to John Jenkins, who was now very confused and not sure of what was happening. She had felt real sadness at parting from him because she owed so much to his kindness. She had also made a visit to Cancoed and this too had left her full of mixed emotions. Her parents had aged, and her father was now crippled with arthritis after all his years of working outside in all weathers. They were struggling to make ends meet on the smallholding but thankfully her brother had taken over all the heavy chores as well as working his own small farm. So much was changing. Looking out of the train window, through clouds of steam, she saw the houses and shops of Newtown as the train slowed and stopped.

Getting off here on this busy summer's day, Margaret noticed that most of the passengers had walked quickly down the hill towards the town, while others were whisked away by friends or relatives in carriages or carts, vanishing down the road in a cloud of dust. Margaret's letter of appointment had included instructions telling her to wait outside the station where she would be collected by the carter. Two other people were also standing outside the station entrance: a young woman looking nervous and anxiously checking the time on the station clock, and a well turned-out gentleman in his thirties who stood to one side as if not wanting to associate with the two young women. Margaret could tell from the cut of his woollen suit and smart leather shoes that this was no countryman. He definitely had the look of the town about him, although he too was clearly anxious as he took out his pocket watch every few minutes or so, studying the dial as if hours could have passed instead of the minute or two since his last inspection. Perhaps they too were bound for Gregynog?

Contenting herself with enjoying the quiet interlude, the warmth of the sunshine and the sound of the bees contentedly buzzing on the honeysuckle behind her, Margaret waited patiently. Life had already taught her that things could rarely be rushed, that there was little to be gained by worrying or imagining the worst. Her way was to take things as they came rather than to try to fight against it or indeed to control it. All that had happened to her over the last ten years had demonstrated that she had absolutely no control over life's events. Just when she was beginning to feel secure and comfortable, the spectre would reappear and send her off along some new path.

Within quarter of an hour, the sound of carriage wheels and the regular hoof beats of a horse could be heard approaching. Drawing to a halt before them, the young man in charge of the vehicle stepped down.

'I'm here from Gregynog. Thomas Owens, carter. Let me have your bags here at the back.'

Thomas Owens was clearly a man of few words, and his speech seemed forced and stilted. Margaret wondered if his first language was Welsh and if that was the reason for his abrupt and terse way of speaking. With the luggage loaded, Margaret and the other young woman sat inside the open carriage, leaving the gentleman to climb up front alongside the carter. Thomas shook the reins and called to the horse and they began to move. Feeling that it would be impossible to spend the journey in silence, Margaret spoke to the woman first.

'I'm Margaret Davies. I'm to be second cook, what will you be doing?'

'Iris Jones, miss, I'm to be a housemaid. Will it be very large, miss, this house?'

The smart young man turned around to address them.

'Idris Hughes, ladies, I am to be valet to the young Master, Charles Hanbury Tracy, as he is to come of age next month and will be requiring his own manservant. To answer your question Iris, yes Gregynog is a large house and a large estate covering many hundreds of acres. I believe there are many acres of woodland, Thomas?'

'Aye, sir, many acres and a saw mill. My brother works in the saw mill, 'tis a big business.'

During the conversation they had driven through the main streets of Newtown, past the market hall where Margaret and Rhiannon had listened to Sybil Thomas, and they were now passing the vast canal basin with its many warehouses and rows of terraced cottages. This part of town was new to Margaret, and she looked around in amazement at the number of barges waiting to unload their cargo of coal or to be loaded with large quantities of woollen goods for the return journey to Chirk. The whole area was noisy and full of activity and bustle. Men were working on the quayside, in the limekilns and in foundries where smoke billowed from chimneys and red sparks shot high into the air. Running around this melee were ragged children and women shouting as they fought for custom for their pies and bread, held aloft in wicker baskets. This cacophony of sound and movement even exceeded her experience, with Rhiannon, of Newtown's Royal Welsh Warehouse!

As the carriage began to climb the hill out of town, the sounds faded until they could be heard no more. At the top of the hill they left all signs of habitation behind and entered the calm of a rural landscape. Soft hills rolled out before them, each crest giving way to another behind, many dotted with clusters of white sheep grazing the lush summer pasture. The track rose and fell many times, twisting and turning to hug the contours of the hills until Margaret could no longer even guess which direction she was facing. After an hour or so they dropped down, and in front of them Margaret could see the roofline of houses and the tall spire of a church. This must be Tregynon.

At the edge of the village Thomas pulled sharply on the reins, and the horse turned left onto a private driveway. They had crossed the threshold of the estate and soon passed a lodge house on the right, followed by a glimpse of a lake and wooden summer house on the left. Either side of the driveway were many trees, the afternoon sunlight flickering between the leaves of oak and ash, beech and birch, chestnut and sycamore, dappling the ground beneath with shimmering patterns.

Suddenly the house was there in front of them, the black-and-white façade standing out starkly against the rich greens of lawns and hedges. The carriage swung round and came to a halt in the centre of the stableyard. Idris Hughes jumped down, opened the door and offered his hand to the two women as they stepped carefully down onto the cobbles. Thomas had unstrapped their bags and – having handed them back to his new colleagues – he gestured to a large wooden door.

'You are to go in through the door and knock on the green door inside. That is Mrs Harris' door. Mrs Harris, the Housekeeper.'

Turning to thank Thomas, Margaret noticed that although he wasn't very tall – barely an inch taller than her – he was stockily built and strong from his outdoor work, and carried himself in an upright and forceful way. He had a square face with a strong chin, emphasised by his bushy sideburns. His dark eyes looked back at her with interest, and he gave a faint smile before turning his attentions to the horse and beginning to unhitch him from the carriage. Margaret returned his smile and then – taking a deep breath – she joined Iris and Mr Idris Hughes as they crossed the cobbles to the rear door of Gregynog Hall.

Chapter 16

STEPPING INTO THE rear hall, they were met by a great wave of heat emanating from the large ovens in the kitchen. Looking from left to right, Margaret could see an enormous kitchen – strange how kitchens just seemed to get bigger and bigger in her life – with three women working away around a sturdy wooden table; to the right there was a passage with many doors and, standing in front of them on the red tiled floor, a huge metal safe with combination lock such as you would see in a bank. She couldn't help but wonder if it was full of the Sudeley's gold and jewels but she would later discover that in fact it contained the family's most precious china and glassware, and was strictly under the control of the butler, Mr Jarvis. Idris Hughes had spotted the green door and rapped smartly with his knuckles.

'Come in,' echoed from the other side of the door and he stood back to allow the two women to enter before him. They found themselves in what appeared to be a small but comfortable sitting room. Mrs Harris, the lady from the interview day in Newtown, sat behind a wooden desk where she had been busy entering figures in her account ledgers.

'Welcome to Gregynog,' she smiled at all of them.

'Mr Hughes, if you would like to come with me, I'll introduce you to Mr Lloyd, who is Lord Sudeley's valet. He will explain your duties to you and show you your quarters.'

She turned to Margaret and Iris. 'I won't be a moment, do sit down.'

They both sat on the wooden chairs that she had gestured towards, and looked around the room with interest.

'It's very big, isn't it?' Iris' voice shook slightly and she was clearly overawed by her surroundings.

'I've worked in other houses,' replied Margaret, 'and each one has been larger than the one before. It's best to forget about the size and just concentrate on the job in front of you. One bed to make or twenty, it's the same job really, you'll see.'

Before they could say anything more, Mrs Harris came back into the room and began to outline their duties. When she had finished, she rose to her feet again and they followed her up the back stairs until they reached the third floor. Here, tucked under the eaves, were the servants' quarters. Opening the door onto a large room containing four iron beds, she pointed to the one in the corner.

'That will be yours, Iris. You will share the room with Megan, another housemaid, and the two kitchen maids, Daisy and Ellen. There is an empty drawer for you in the chest. Now go and unpack your belongings and then make your way back down the stairs to the servants' hall next to the kitchen, as tea will be served at five o'clock.'

She then led Margaret further along the corridor before opening a door to a smaller room, similarly equipped with an iron bedstead. Here, though, there was just one bed, a small chest of drawers and an old easy chair. The window was framed with blue floral curtains and looked out over the gardens and to the woods beyond. Although not a true window seat, the ledge was both low and wide enough to sit on, and Margaret was drawn to it, already loving the view that was hers alone.

Immediately behind the house she could see well-tended vegetable gardens, chicken runs and fruit trees. There would be plenty of home-grown produce. Looking past the gardens to the rolling hills beyond, patches of woodland, beech and birch, strong oaks and chestnut trees stood proudly, their leaves moving gently with the wind. It was a view that would change with the seasons, with the time of day and would bring something new to gaze upon whenever she had the chance to sit there. Running below the window was a large metal pipe, some six inches in diameter. It entered through the left wall, ran the width of the room, and exited again through the right side. Seeing her puzzled expression, Mrs Harris smiled,

'It's for the heating, Mrs Davies. Lord Sudeley had pipes and radiators fitted throughout the house just a few years ago, and we have a large boiler in the brick building out there, which heats the water before it circulates around the house. It is very ingenious, if a little temperamental. You don't have a radiator but the pipe gets very warm in winter and stops the rooms becoming really chilled.'

Margaret smiled, already anticipating the luxury during the winter months.

'Thank you. I'm Miss Davies, though, not Mrs. I have never been married.'

'I understand, but as one of the cooks you will be known as Mrs. I too have never been married but it's traditional for all senior ladies of the household to be known as Mrs. You are working for the gentry now, and that is the way things are.'

'Oh well, I don't suppose it matters. I'm sure I shall get used to it. Should I unpack my things now?'

'Yes, do that and then join us in the servants' hall. You have had a long day and must be needing some food and a cup of tea. You'll find your uniform dresses and aprons hanging behind the curtain there. Are you good with a needle, should they need any altering? You sent your measurements so they should be fine; no need to wear them until tomorrow.'

With that she left the room, closing the door gently behind her, and Margaret moved again to the window. She felt a frisson of excitement run down her spine at the thought of this new world that she had entered. Before going down for her meal, she took a quick look at the dresses, and there were indeed two smart black uniforms with a selection of aprons, heavy cotton for dirty work and then three white trimmed aprons for meetings with Lady Sudeley. She couldn't wait to try them on; she imagined that she would look quite different to the young woman who had started out as kitchen maid to John Jenkins.

Chapter 17

THE HEAT IN the kitchens had long passed the point where anyone could work comfortably. All four ovens were full of bread and pies, cakes and roasting meat. Every available space on the hob was covered with heavy copper pans of all sizes and shapes. Whole carp and salmon steamed in fish kettles, sauces thickened to a glossy finish in flat bottomed pans, vegetables simmered and fruit stewed in order to feed the thousands of people expected the following day. At four in the afternoon, Margaret wiped the sweat from her hairline for the hundredth time and wished again that Master Charles had been a winter baby.

The preparations had been underway for days; there had been many hours of planning, for which Mrs Edwards, the cook, Margaret, Lady Sudeley and Mr Jarvis the butler had all sat in the morning room and discussed the options for the main dinner for the house party, and the afternoon tea for two and a half thousand people, which included all the village, estate workers, the official party from the hall and many guests from the well-to-do and important persons from Newtown. Margaret had sat quietly for the most part through these meetings, feeling too unsure of herself to offer her opinions, merely taking notes as the menus were decided and the wine lists complied along with choices for the vast quantities of ale and cider for the afternoon amusements.

Hearing her name called, she turned, lifting her gaze from the pan in front of her.

'Mrs Davies, you can leave that sauce to Daisy for a moment, she is quite able to watch it thicken. You must take a break; you haven't stopped since early morning. Come to my sitting room and take a cup of tea with me.'

The window was open in the small room and a wonderful breeze lifted the light muslin curtains. This was Margaret's first invitation to Cook's sitting room and she felt a little nervous but so relieved to be out of the heat of the kitchen for a short while.

'Sit down, take that easy chair and rest for a minute. I'll say this for you, you're no shirker. I wasn't sure when you arrived, you looked no older than some of the maids, but you've a good head on your shoulders and you only ever need to be asked once. I'm very glad to have you, with all this extra work going on.'

Lifting the delicate china teapot, she poured two cups of tea, added milk and a spoonful of sugar to each cup before passing one to Margaret.

'Thank you, I didn't realise how tired I was until I sat down. It's the heat. I don't mind hard work but the temperature in the kitchen today is unbearable.'

'Have a shortbread biscuit, I make them myself in the evenings. I like to have a biscuit with my tea, Cook's perk!'

The two women ate and drank in silence for a few minutes, content to be off their feet and enjoying the fresh air blowing across their faces.

'Tomorrow will be a long day. After the meal at one o'clock, there will be the tea to lay out. We have about ten women from the village coming in to help so our role will be to direct the whole thing from the kitchen.'

'I feel as if I've been making cakes for weeks,' sighed Margaret. 'I always loved baking, especially a fruit cake, but now I'd be happy never to see another one as long as I live! I've never been a part of anything like this before. I can't imagine how much it is all going to cost.'

With a snort and a roll of her eyes, Mary Edwards leaned forward in a conspiratorial manner.

'No doubt, we'll never see a figure but it will run into thousands, and rumour has it that they can't really afford it. You mark my words, it will be cheap cuts and plain cooking once this is all over. It was almost two years ago that Miss Eva got married and you've never seen such celebrations. And now we're doing it all over again! Lord Sudeley has spent so much money over the last few years – doing up the properties on the estate, getting the saw mill modernised and into production – that you have to wonder where it all comes from. I heard Mrs Harris and Mr Jarvis talking, and they were saying that Lady Sudeley has had to use her own money to pay for this birthday celebration, so they must be feeling the pinch. We can only hope that life settles down after this and things return to normal.'

Margaret's eyes had widened at being included in this revelation. She had quite innocently believed that, for people such as the Sudeleys, money was never an issue. She imagined some sort of inexhaustible supply, about as far removed from her meagre wages and hidden savings as could ever be dreamed of.

'But surely, if they do not have enough money, they wouldn't organise something on this scale?'

Cook laughed. 'Bless you dear, the gentry don't work like that. It's all about appearances, you see. Lord Sudeley must be seen to be wealthy. He's MP for these parts, has business interests in the Cambrian Mills and this huge estate. It wouldn't do for folk to think he was struggling. I like His Lordship and Lady Sudeley – they're good employers, always treat the staff fair, they do – but something will give before too long, you wait and see. I've seen it before with other families, sooner or later these things come to a head.'

The day of the birthday came and went; the weather was kind to the local gentry and the estate workers alike after some early showers, and all the planned events took place without disruption. It was late in the afternoon before Margaret finally left the kitchen, and she wandered through the gardens watching the children laughing at the Punch and Judy show, the youngsters on the swing boats and coconut shy. Many of the older ladies and men from the village sat around on blankets, enjoying a rare break from work and getting pleasure from the antics of the young folk around them. Replete with tea and cake, scones and sandwiches, they were content to observe, to gossip and mull over the day and all they had seen. The highlight of the day had been the singing troupe blacked up in minstrel make-up and singing shanty songs from the Deep South.

As she turned the corner of the rose garden, intending to walk into the woods – not caring about the light drizzle which had started to fall – she caught sight of Thomas Owens leading two ponies back to the stable. There had been many horse races that afternoon and it wasn't surprising to see that he had been involved. With a halter in each hand, he stood still to let her pass. Unable to lift his hat, he offered a tentative smile.

'Have you seen much of the amusements?' he asked.

'Not really. I've been in the kitchen, baking scones and slicing cake after cake. I am sick of cake!'

Her words made him smile, as though he wasn't used to such forthright speech from young women. Margaret had learned from Thomas that his family were poor; they all worked for the Gregynog estate in one capacity or another, and there never seemed to be quite enough of anything to go round. She could well believe that he found the crowded family home a difficult place to be as he loved open spaces and enjoyed the tranquillity of the estate just as she did.

'Well, I had some fruit cake so if that was your baking, it was really good. I have to get these two back to the stables now. Enjoy your walk.'

'Thank you, it will be good to be a bit quieter now, although I expect there will be a great deal of clearing up to do tomorrow. If there's any cake left, I'll make sure some gets put to one side for the gardeners and stable lads, for you and the other men when you take your break. Good night.'

She walked slowly off beneath the trees, aware that Thomas was standing, watching her leave. It had been a long day and she had been on her feet for twelve hours or more but she walked steadily with her back straight and head high. Margaret glanced back a moment and noticed that Thomas' gaze lingered for a few more minutes before he turned towards the stables.

Chapter 18

THE SUN WAS dropping from the sky, turning the air around it a delicate shade of pink. Margaret sat at her window seat, softened now by patchwork cushions she had sewn during the long winter evenings. She had enjoyed the last two years at Gregynog, especially the camaraderie in the kitchens, the busy days filled with chatter and laughter as she had learned new skills and expanded her repertoire of dishes. Mrs Edwards' judgement back at the time of the young master's birthday celebrations had been correct. There had been many economies made afterwards: requests for more simple meals had arrived in the kitchens, some of the rooms had been closed through the winter months and fewer fires were lit. On the estate, too, many workers had been dismissed, and as a result many young families had left the area. Both rich and poor were feeling the effects of hard times, and through the harshest period of the winter of 1894, Mrs Scott Owen and Lady Sudeley had provided a soup kitchen in the village for those who could hardly afford to eat themselves or feed their children. For the workers who still had jobs, times were also hard, as they worked long days to complete all the tasks required of them with less manpower.

Cook had beckoned Margaret in to her sitting room when it was time for their mid-morning break. Closing the door carefully behind her, she moved across to swing her small kettle over the fire, moving gently despite her size. Margaret looked out of the small window and enjoyed the sight of the old trees swaying in the wind. It was much quieter here than in the kitchen, the only sound was that of the birds singing and the occasional call of one gardener to another as they moved along the flowerbeds, removing weeds and dead-heading dozens of roses.

'Come and sit down.' Cook handed Margaret a cup of tea with the usual fresh biscuit placed on the saucer. 'We will know today what's going on. His Lordship has been going around with a long face for days and there have been endless visitors; solicitor was here, and the bank manager. It's not looking good but at least we'll find out soon.'

Margaret took a long sip from her tea as if needing the sustenance.

'Surely it can't be that bad? The Sudeleys are a wealthy family and – just because he's no longer Member of Parliament – that doesn't make him poor.'

'No, but there's more gone wrong than we know about, you mark my words. None of the accounts have been paid for the last six months and Roberts the Butchers are already grumbling about the outstanding bills.'

'Do you think that something serious is going to be announced? Will we all lose our jobs?'

'I don't know about that Margaret, but I do know that Lady Sudeley does not look well. She has aged something cruel over these last few months.'

Leaning closer she lowered her voice. 'Mrs Harris told me that she had heard them – Lord and Lady – having a right royal argument, and that Lady Sudeley had turned on him and accused him of losing all her money. Now if that's the case, they are scraping the barrel. They're laying off folk from the Cambrian Mill, they can't make the cloth as fast or as cheap as the mills up north, and he's done nothing but spend his money here for the last few years. Always got to be having a celebration, some sort of showing off and now look where it's going to end!'

Margaret felt her insides turn to jelly and the old fears of change began to quiver in her stomach. She loathed the fact that so little in her life came under her own influence and control. Was she always to remain at the mercy of the decisions of her betters?

The two women went back to their work and, sure enough, they were interrupted less than an hour later with a message from the butler that everyone should assemble in the servants' hall at midday.

The room was full, as all the outdoor workers had also been gathered, and Margaret could see Thomas standing quietly at the rear, alongside his father and brother. The whispers and mumblings faded to silence as the door opened, and in walked Lord Sudeley and Mr Scott Owen.

The first to speak was Lord Sudeley, his face white and tense. 'It is my duty to speak to you all here today, and thank you for the loyal and excellent service you have performed for me and my family over the years. Sadly, I also have to inform you that Her Ladyship and I will shortly be leaving Gregynog Hall, to live with a much reduced household in Surrey. I have experienced some business difficulties which have resulted in me losing large sums of money and, because of that, Gregynog Hall is to be sold.'

There was a collective in-drawn breath at this announcement and, as His Lordship left the room, a gentle murmur of questions began slowly to rise. Before the conversations could erupt, Mr Scott Owen cleared his throat and waited for silence to resume.

'This is a sad day for all concerned, but it is my job now to give you all as much information about the future as I am able. Gregynog Hall will be going up for sale when a suitable purchaser can be found but, in the meantime, His Lordship has agreed a loan against the property, so putting it into the hands of Economic Life, the insurance company. The decision has been taken to rent out the hall as a country house with the usual shooting, hunting and fishing rights, and the new tenant will be Sir John Rigby.'

At this announcement feet were shuffled and looks exchanged, some of relief that there would still be tenants, if not owners at Gregynog. Perhaps things would not be too bad after all?

'It would appear that Sir John will not live in the hall for the whole year, merely during the hunting season and will therefore only require a small indoor staff. Please listen carefully for your name so that you know what is to be your new role, if any.'

The mood shifted and everyone stood quietly, waiting for the axe to fall where it would, leaving them employed or both out of work and without a home. As Mr Scott Owen began to read through the list, all that could be heard were soft sighs of relief and low moans of despair.

Among the indoor staff, the housekeeper, Mrs Harris, the senior cook, Mrs Edwards and the butler, Mr Jarvis, were all leaving for Surrey with the Sudeleys. To her great relief, Margaret was offered the post of cook/housekeeper to Sir John Rigby at Gregynog, the two kitchen maids would also remain, along with the most senior footman, David Thomas. Everyone else would have to seek new positions. As far as the outside staff were concerned, all would continue to be employed for the present time, as the horses would still need to be cared for, gardens attended to and the game reared for the hunting season.

Mr Scott Owen collected together his papers and thanked them for their attention. As he moved towards the door, he hesitated before speaking again.

'If it's any consolation, I am saddened beyond words at what has happened and that I, along with His Lordship, have failed to be able to secure the house and all your positions. You will all receive two weeks' pay and glowing references. Thank you, now best return to your work.'

Having served afternoon tea for the Sudeleys, Margaret continued to slice and butter bread, lay out jam and cheese and slices of ginger cake for the servants' tea, all the while her mind churning with the day's revelations. Tea was normally a quiet meal, everyone needing to rest after a long day's work, but today the room was full of chatter and exclamation.

'I've no idea where I shall go,' cried Iris. 'I've loved working here and now it's all over. We only have a week and we must be gone. I shall have to go home to my mother again while I look for a new post and she will blame me, I know she will. She always does. At least I shall have a reference this time.'

'We're all in the same boat, Iris,' Megan said. 'We must ask Thomas to bring back a newspaper from Newtown and we can see what jobs are around. I think I shall head north and change direction entirely. There are many new opportunities now in shops and factories, banks and offices. I've had enough of clearing up after rich folk and then getting dropped when they don't need you any more. No more life in service for me!'

'Now, now,' said Cook, from the end of the table. 'Things are going to be different for us all, and you young ones will soon find work. I don't know how it will be for me in Surrey; it will only be a small house and I think we shall be doing all kinds of work.' Turning to the housekeeper Mrs Harris, who was also moving, she added, 'I don't know about you, but I'm getting too old for scrubbing floors and washing up. Oh, what will become of us all?'

Slowly, they all finished the simple meal and returned to their duties, bodies working automatically while their heads tried to process the news. Margaret mused – with a little bitterness – on the unfairness of her old friend, Change, turning up again, just as she had got comfortable in her life and her work.

Sitting later in the evening light, she picked up the letter which had been delivered that morning from her sister. Lizzie and she exchanged letters regularly but this one had left her with a heavy heart as it brought news that her mam was unwell. Lizzie wrote of repeated bouts of fever and a bad chest which had weakened their mother considerably. She could no longer cope with running Cancoed. As the crow flies, Margaret was probably only twenty-five miles away but it may as well have been a thousand, for there was little she could do to help. If she resigned from her position and went home, she would just be another person to feed and house, so she had to stay. In staying, she could see that there would be fewer opportunities for making the journey home as her role was to entail greater responsibilities.

She crossed to the chest and took out her writing paper and

pen, ink and envelopes (her leaving gift from John Jenkins and family), and began a reply to Lizzie. Along with sympathy and many heartfelt wishes and hopes for her mother's recovery she outlined the changes at Gregynog. Searching for something positive to share, she mentioned her growing friendship with Thomas Owens.

I have a new friend here at Gregynog, Thomas Owens. He is the carter, and takes great care of all the horses and ponies. We have taken some evening walks together. He is very knowledgeable about all the trees and plants that grow here. He lives in a small cottage on the estate and has four chickens and a pig he is fattening up. She is called Mabel. I think he will regret giving her a name when it is time for her to be killed. I see him on Sundays, after chapel. He always sits with his family, there are eleven brothers and sisters and they fill two whole pews.

If I am able to take my weekend leave next month, I shall come home on the train. I feel sure that Thomas would take me down to the station in Newtown if I tell him that Mam is so poorly.

Once Lord and Lady Sudeley had left, taking with them many pieces of furniture, paintings, china and rugs, Gregynog seemed bereft. A house without a family is just a house and not a home. With fewer people in the building, the sounds of pipes gurgling and the squeaks of floorboards became more noticeable, and Margaret found herself continuously looking over her shoulder as she worked through the day.

However, since Sir John was not planning to move in any of his personal effects for a month or so, and had requested that there be a thorough cleaning of the hall, a list had been compiled of any repairs or renovations needed, whose contents fell to Margaret to address and oversee. In her new post as housekeeper, Margaret was relishing the freedom to explore the house at her leisure.

One wet morning at the end of the summer, she decided to turn her attention to the condition of all the rugs and curtains in the main bedrooms of the house, and she and Megan left the kitchen with pen, paper and a measuring tape.

'We'll take the front stairs, Megan, they lead directly to the main bedrooms and there's no one to be upset by it. Come on, now.'

Together they started up the beautifully curved staircase, moulded from concrete, with its channelled handrail. The two women followed the bend to the first floor, their hands lightly resting in the hollow of the concrete.

'I don't know how they made this, Mrs Davies, but it's very beautiful. It feels as if it was just made for my hand. Isn't it smooth?'

'It is, and as you say, very clever, but we have work to do, so we'd best get on with it, not stand around admiring things.'

Chapter 19

L IFE AT GREGYNOG continued. The warmth of summer followed the frosts and snow of winter and the house had its own cycle, periods of bustle and noise, activity and long hours of work when Sir John and his guests were in residence, followed by long months of quiet and isolation as the skeleton staff kept things ticking over in readiness for the next shooting season. It felt strange to sit around the small table to take their meals, only half a dozen full-time members of staff now instead of the twelve or more from the time of the Sudeleys.

*

The hall had been full throughout the autumn and into January, but now the season was closed and Sir John and the last of his guests had departed that morning. Margaret walked through the rooms after they had left, making notes about what needed mending or cleaning, which ornaments would need careful washing and wrapping before the dust sheets were replaced for another eight months. She had come to a standstill in what had been Lady Sudeley's bedroom as she looked out over the gardens; her shoulders dropped as she felt the tension of the last months slip from her and she fancied that the house, too, took a sigh of relief before settling more comfortably onto its beams and rafters.

She had caught sight of Thomas walking down the back lane towards the stables with a barrowload of hay and – on the spur of the moment – she pulled up her skirts and took off down the back stairs. She reached the back door and hurried outside, calling to him as he turned the corner into the tack room.

'Thomas, do you have a minute?' She was panting by the time she reached his side and he held open the door for her, indicating an old stool, where she sank down with gratitude. The door closed behind her and, the cold wind blocked, she felt the warmth from the old fire place and was comforted by the smells of leather and saddle soap, hay and horse, which filled the small room.

'Are you all right, Margaret?' Thomas reached out a hand, touching her shoulder with concern.

'I am, thank you, but I saw you from the upstairs window and it seems so long since we had time to talk that I thought it would be good to take five minutes. We have worked so hard, Thomas, I'm sure you and the others outside have, too. It's certainly not like the old days. Those friends of Sir John's are nothing like Lord and Lady Sudeley's guests.'

Thomas nodded, 'Aye, you can say that right enough. They hammer the horses and care nothing for how tired the hounds get.'

'I can imagine. They have filled every room inside, and the dirt! You cannot imagine the dirt, they walk through the corridors in their muddy boots instead of removing them at the door, they throw their filthy hunting clothes down onto the rugs and the beds, causing so much work. My poor girls are exhausted. I am glad to see the back of them.' Margaret was seldom critical: it was as though she needed this release, following such hard work.

'The only good thing to come out of it is that there's more work for the families from the village. I had to put on extra beaters and grooms. How many did you take on inside?'

'Five women, three just to cope with the laundry and the other two helped in the kitchen. There has been so much cooking to be done, and so many of the guests brought along a manservant, not that they seemed to do much work, just created extra mouths to feed, as far as I could see. But you're right, it has at least put money in the hands of local folk for a few months.'

She stood slowly, shook out her dress and turned to go. 'Thank you for listening, I just had to get some of that anger off my chest. I shall be fine now.'

She smiled and some of her old sparkle returned to her eyes, although her face still looked tired and drawn.

'I'll see you later in the hall, for tea. It will be quiet then and for once we can all sit down and enjoy our break.'

With that, she had left the tack room, exchanging its equine warmth for the cold air outside, before passing quickly through the back door and returning to her work.

The first day of peace and serenity ended as always with tea and, as everyone finished their meal, Margaret stood up with the large brown tea pot and enquired, 'Would anyone like some more?'

She moved around the table, refilling cups, passing milk and sugar, urging them to eat up the last slices of ginger cake.

'Thank you, all of you, for your hard work. The house will have to be cleaned and tidied away as we did last year, but the next few days are to be rest days. We shall do the minimum of work. Megan and Daisy, I don't expect to see you down here before seven in the morning. An extra hour in bed will do you both good. Breakfast will be at eight.' She turned to Thomas and asked, 'Will that be all right for you and the lad? Could you also tell the gardeners, please?' Then back to the servant household, 'Now let's clear up here and no more work today. You can spend the evening doing whatever you wish, girls.'

The sky was already dark but Margaret felt an urge to be outside, to breathe in fresh air rather than cooking smells and cigar fumes. Wrapping her coat tightly around her, she pulled an old shawl over her head and shoulders and slipped out of the back door, across the cobbles of the stable yard and into the gardens. It was too late to head for the woods, but she walked briskly around the gravelled paths that separated the flowerbeds. There was little to be seen at this time of year, but in the months to come they would be ablaze with the colour and the scent of roses and delphiniums, lavender and rosemary, hollyhocks and lupins. On this chilly, frosty evening the only flowers brave enough to push their way through the dark loamy soil were the snowdrops. Small clusters sat beneath the hedges, as if hoping for some comfort or shelter, glistening in the light of the early moon.

Reaching the driveway, she gained speed and followed the track until she reached the lodge. Lamps were lit in the house and – through the leaded windows – she could see the gamekeeper and his wife and children seated around the table. He, too, would be tired, as much of the work of the shoot had fallen on his shoulders. From the kennels at the rear of the house she could hear low sounds from the dogs, restless no doubt, as they would have missed their exercise today. And so, it would begin again, another round of bird rearing, dog training, and all for another four months of slaughter until there would be few pheasants or ducks left on the estate, fewer rabbits and hares and many less salmon and trout in the rivers. She was a countrywoman through and through, but she still found it hard to come to terms with blood sport. To kill to put food on the table she could understand, to kill for the fun of it left her sickened.

As she turned at the end of the gardens to retrace her steps, she saw Thomas standing by the large oak tree. He had been waiting for her. He had been watching her walk back towards the house.

'I'm glad you're back, Margaret. I don't like to think of you walking alone after dark. Take my arm and I'll walk with you back to the house.'

'Thank you. I just had to get some air this evening, to feel the wind in my hair. We have been so busy for so many weeks that it's been all I could do at the end of each day to climb the stairs to my room.'

'I know, but it will be quiet now, anyroad. No noise and excitement for a while. The horses will be glad of a rest, they are all worn out and I've one lame, so the blacksmith will be here in the morning to check his shoes.'

'How are things at the cottage now? Are you settled there with the animals?'

'I am, but sometimes it is lonely, some company would be good.' He paused, looking down at his own shoes, then added, 'Will you be coming to chapel on Sunday? Mam has asked if you would like to come home with me for tea afterwards. What do you think?'

In the darkness, Margaret's cheeks grew warm. She knew only too well the significance of this invitation. It would be wrong of her to give Thomas encouragement if she wasn't serious about him. Neither of them were young; he was thirty-seven to her thirty-four. She had had her taste of romance with Walter, and that had ended in disaster. She had no great desire to end her days as a lonely old woman, and her role at Gregynog was far from secure in the current situation. Holding his arm tightly, she gave it a squeeze before replying, 'I'd like that, Thomas. Thank your mam for me and tell her I'd be pleased to come.'

They had reached the back door and, as he opened it, Thomas turned her towards him and placed a gentle kiss on her cheek.

'That will be grand, I will be proud to introduce you to the family. Good night, *cariad*.'

And with that, he pushed her gently but firmly through the door and waited for the key to be turned and the two bolts to slide into place. With a wide smile on his normally solemn face, he whistled up his dog and set off down the lane to Tŷ'n-y-Coed.

Inside the house, Margaret touched her fingers to her cheek and thought, not for the first time, of married life with Thomas. She was no innocent, but he had accepted her past when she had shared with him the story of her first love, of her rejection and of young Teddy's short life. He had held her hand and listened, his only judgement being reserved for Walter and his family. In accepting his invitation this evening, it would be understood by everyone that they were now 'walking out' and that sometime soon this would be followed by a wedding. Making her way to her room, she wondered if she would be blessed with another child one day. She knew that she and Thomas would not be well off; she knew that she would have to resign her post as housekeeper and would no longer be independent, but if she could hold a healthy child in her arms again one day, then the sacrifice would be worth it. She and Thomas were friends, they liked each other and she was confident that they could grow to love each other. This was not the giddy rush of young love but the practical joining of two lonely people who could support each other through whatever lay ahead.

Chapter 20

T HE WEDDING WAS to be a simple affair, as was the case for most ordinary people at this time. At the beginning of May Margaret had paid a visit to Mr Scott Owen's house and asked to speak with him. After a few moments left standing in the hallway with little to look at but some heavily framed pictures of religious scenes, Margaret had turned on hearing his voice, 'Mrs Davies, please come in to my study.'

She had followed him in to a book-lined room with oak furniture and windows dressed with heavy drapes, reminiscent of John Jenkins' study back in Llanidloes. After exchanging pleasantries, she had produced an envelope, addressed in her neat writing to him as estate manager.

'I'm sorry, sir, but it is my resignation. I am to be married in just a few weeks.'

'Congratulations. Are the village rumours correct? Is the gentleman in question Thomas Owens?'

'Yes, it is, sir. He has spoken to the farm manager about me joining him at Tŷ'n-y-Coed. It will make a fine home for us, sir. It's only small but I shall soon have it as neat and clean as a new pin.'

'I don't doubt it, and of course you have my blessing. It will be hard to lose you, though; you have been a tower of strength over the last few years. You have been an excellent employee.

Perhaps we may call upon you, though, from time to time, when the hall is busy?'

'Thank you, sir. I have loved living and working at the hall, it's a wonderful place but things haven't been the same since Lord and Lady Sudeley left.'

'I know, we all felt their loss most keenly. We can only hope that before too long the estate may find a new owner and Gregynog will see a new family in residence. It needs to be a home again. But none of that must concern you now, you have much to celebrate. When is the wedding to be?'

'On Friday the twenty-second, sir, at the Methodist chapel in Llanidloes. That is my home chapel and where I wish to be married. If I may leave on the Wednesday, sir, as it is Thomas' half-day and he will take me to the station. It will give me time to visit my family, and I have a room promised at Penygreen for two nights.'

'That will be quite in order. I shall see about placing an advertisement in the *Montgomeryshire Express* for your position. Things are quiet now, and I imagine that you will have already cleaned and prepared the house. Would you be able to write a list for me of your many duties? Your role has changed greatly in the years that you have been here and no one will know more about it than you do.'

She had left Mr Scott Owen, relieved that the meeting was over and had gone well. There was little left for her to do at the hall, and Daisy and Ellen could easily manage to cook for the servants' hall until a new housekeeper could be found.

The end of the winter had brought with it much sadness. Her mother had slipped away one cold February night, the constant coughing and laboured breathing had finally sapped the last vestiges of her strength. Just a week later, a second letter had arrived from John Davies at Penygreen: his uncle, John Jenkins, had also died. The letter gave details of the funeral and included ten guineas, a bequest from the old man for the young lady he had helped some ten years previously. Margaret had shed tears for both of them; two people who had only ever shown her love and support, who had reached out to offer help in whatever ways they could. She held on to the thought that her mam would now be with Teddy, and they would both be content again.

The final paragraph of John Davies' letter had contained his assurance to always to be of help, as they were truly indebted to her for the care given to the old man in his later years. She had kept the letter folded in her savings tin, and once she and Thomas had set a date for the wedding, she had written to ask if they could find space for her to stay for the two nights before her wedding, an attic room would suffice.

*

On the Saturday before the wedding, Thomas harnessed the grey pony to the trap for a drive to Newtown. As the wedding was to be quiet, without fuss and celebration, they had decided to splash out instead by visiting the photographer's studio and have portraits taken to celebrate this milestone in their lives. As she had entered the stable yard, Margaret felt self-conscious and shy.

Thomas coughed and cleared his throat again, twisting his hat in his hands. 'Margaret, fach, you look so lovely. Everything about you is shining.'

He reached out to touch the cameo brooch at her neck; he

had given the trinket to her when she had accepted his clumsy marriage proposal.

'Well, I don't want my picture taken unless I'm looking my best now, do I?' Her brusque words covered her nervousness but she smiled, 'And for goodness' sake stop wringing the life out of that hat, it won't be fit to wear!'

She climbed up on to the cart and Thomas settled by her side. She felt pleased now that she had gone to all the trouble to prepare for the day. The previous evening, she had pressed her smartest dress and fixed the cameo onto the collar. When all the staff had retired to their rooms, she had heated many pans of water and – having locked the doors to the kitchen – she lowered herself into the tin bath and soaked in the hot water until her skin had begun to wrinkle. Having washed her hair, she had rinsed it with vinegar to make it shine. Thomas could see the rich colours glinting in her dark hair. She may have felt unsure about this new phase, but to the world, and to Thomas, she looked every inch a confident and successful woman.

Thomas had done his best to be smart. His working life was not one that called for fine clothes and a groomed appearance, but in honour of the occasion, his sister had trimmed his hair and bushy moustache and sideburns. There had been no soak in a hot bath for him but he had washed at his scullery sink, lathered up his face, sharpened his razor on the leather strop and carefully shaved his cheeks and chin, avoiding his sideburns and moustache. He was wearing his best Sunday clothes, a stiff white collar and a burgundy cravat.

After stealing sideways glances at each other Margaret suddenly laughed. 'What a pair we are, fine clothes don't change us at all, Thomas. Let's get these pictures done and then we can take a walk along the High Street. I've a few spare shillings in my bag so we can see if that tea shop is still there. I told you, the one I went to with Rhiannon.'

Thoughts of her friend and where she might now be wiped the smile from her face for a few moments. The letters had stopped coming and she knew that there was little to be gained from dwelling on what she couldn't change.

They spent the remainder of the journey in companionable quiet except for pointing out the flowers in the hedgerow, the antics of the lambs. Margaret relaxed with the gentle motion of the horse and the creak of the wheels, feeling proud of the way that Thomas controlled the animal, gently but firmly, his deep voice giving occasional words of encouragement.

Chapter 21

THE DOOR TO the chapel was open and Margaret paused to make certain that her ears were not deceiving her. She could hear organ music and she knew that she and Thomas hadn't arranged for this additional cost. John Davies, her host for the past two nights, smiled, tucked her arm through his and opened the door wider.

'We wanted you to have a wedding you would remember fondly, Margaret.'

As the organist became aware of their presence, she changed the music and the unmistakeable notes of Wagner's 'Bridal Chorus' coursed through the building. Margaret stepped forward and together they walked into the chapel and made their way to the front, where Thomas and his brother Ted stood waiting.

John Davies and his wife had prepared a simple single bedroom for her stay, and when she had returned from her visit to Cancoed, saddened to realise that her father's health would not allow him to attend the wedding ceremony, John had stepped in to the breach, asking if he could have the honour of giving her away. They had brushed aside all her protestations and insisted on also providing a simple meal after the service before their return journey home to Tregynon.

It had felt strange to be in the chapel with so few people; usually for Sunday services, every seat would be filled and the sound of the hymn-singing would reach high into the roof space, filling every nook and cranny with the powerful words and haunting tunes. Today, their voices echoed, seeming to rebound off the walls and stained-glass windows. Margaret's sister Lizzie was there, but her sister, Ann, had been unable to attend, as she was soon to have a child. Ted, Thomas' brother, was his best man and represented the Owens family as there wasn't enough money to have allowed them all to travel by train from Newtown to Llanidloes. A small group of ladies sat at the back of the chapel, there just to pass the time, to be the first with news of the latest wedding or funeral. Their comments could be equally scathing on the bride's appearance or the quality of a coffin, particularly if no invitation to wedding meal or funeral tea was offered to them.

As the Reverend Martin blessed them both, Margaret realised that the service was over. She was now a married woman and bound to Thomas for the rest of her life. She had made her vows, held out her hand and been aware of the gold band being placed on her finger, but all of it had passed as if at a distance. She had been there but not really present, observing events as if from above. The minister's final words brought her back into her body, into reality and into the beginning of the next phase of her life.

The remainder of the day passed in a blur; they had eaten dainty sandwiches, each one a mere mouthful for Thomas and Ted, drunk tea from the delicate china cups she remembered so well and finally cut into a dark, moist fruit cake, releasing the aromas of spice and rum. This had almost proved her undoing, as it reminded her so much of her mother, but somehow, she had choked back the tears and smiled and chatted, concealing her emotions as best she could. Finally, goodbyes had been said and they had left Penygreen and walked back through the town to the station.

Glad to be finally free from the constraints of chapel and then the big house at Penygreen, Thomas reached for her hand, 'Hello Mrs Owens, are you all right?'

She smiled back at him, linking her arm through his as they climbed the hill.

'I am, I'm just fine. Wasn't it kind of the Davieses to lay on the food and the organ in chapel? I hadn't been expecting all that.'

'It was indeed, they must think a good deal of you, Margaret. Look, our train is there, we'd best hurry.'

They settled into their seats and – as the rhythm of the engine rocked their carriage – Margaret was lulled into a state midway between sleep and wakefulness. She watched the last houses fade from view, and knew that there would be few chances of returning to Llanidloes. Her new role as wife – and hopefully mother – would take up all her hours and there would be no spare money for luxuries like train tickets. As was expected, she had told Thomas of her small savings and placed the money in a joint cash box which by now was waiting at Tŷ'n-y-coed; some of it had already been earmarked for the purchase of a cow, and he had agreed that she may wish to make curtains and rag rugs for the cottage. Only Margaret knew that she had kept back five pounds, it was knotted into a handkerchief and hidden amongst her underclothes. She had been an independent woman for too long to hand over every hard-earned penny, and just knowing that the money was hers seemed to help in the transition to this new life. She had no illusions as to how hard life was likely to be, and for that reason it was very important to her to retain some small level of control. As the train jerked and began to slow, she smiled at Thomas sitting opposite her, grateful for his silence and lack of questions.

Waiting at the station was William, Thomas' father and now her father-in-law. She supposed she would be seeing much more of him now that she would be a part of the family and that he worked with Thomas every day, preparing the horses for whatever work was needed. Before leaving for Llanidloes, Thomas had taken the box containing all her treasured possessions to Tŷ'n-y-coed, and now she felt excited to be going home to the cottage and the next few days when she could begin to make her mark on the little house.

'So, you're married then: I have myself a new daughter-in-law,' the old man's lined face crinkled into a smile and Margaret went willingly to kiss his cheek. She had grown to like and respect William, his hard-working ways and the kindness he always showed to his wife.

'We are indeed, and I'm sure this new husband of mine will be wanting a dinner soon, all those tiny bites in Llanidloes won't have filled him for long.'

They chatted amongst themselves as the cart made the journey back uphill to Tregynon. It may only have been forty-eight hours since she left, but Margaret was returning with a new name, a new life and a new home.

The cart pulled in at Gregynog stables and she and Thomas dismounted, thanked both Ted and William for their support, and set off on the final leg of their journey. Tŷ'n-y-coed could only be reached by foot or on horseback, and as they took the lower back drive from the hall, crossed the river and headed up the hill on a dusty track, the reality of her new situation became clear to Margaret. On this warm May evening, the fields were awash with campion and buttercups, while celandines and dandelions carpeted the meadow alongside the river, and small clumps of yellow Welsh poppies burst into bloom under the hedges. The well-trodden path was dry and firm beneath their feet but as she looked down at the grooves in the dry ground, she wondered what it would be like to walk in mid-winter after days of rain or even snow. Quickly shaking the negative thoughts from her mind, she turned to her new husband.

'We're nearly home, Thomas. I can't wait to settle in and start to make it more homely for you. You must have been lonely all the way out here with no one to talk to. Look, I can see the chimney now!'

Thomas reached for her hand, twining their fingers together, pulled her to him and kissed her more roughly, more passionately than ever before. He looked longingly at her, his eyes grown dark with desire. It surely must be true that he had been lonely living so far away from the hall and the other staff, so far from the warmth and company he had been used to in his family home, but it wasn't conversation he had been longing for.

'Come on then, woman, we've more important things to be doing than talking about carpets and cushions. I'll race you to the top.'

As he uttered the last few words, he began to quicken his pace, breaking into a run and leaving his new bride behind him. Surprised by his quick action, Margaret lifted her skirts and broke into a run. Her work had made her fit, and she was carrying no spare weight so she was soon close behind him, never quite catching him but reaching the door of the cottage only seconds behind him. Hot, flushed and giddy with the impromptu fun after the solemnity of the day, they pushed open the door. Thomas dropped the bag which had held her overnight things, took her hand and led her straight to the small bedroom under the eaves.

Thomas' experiences had been confined to a few outdoor couplings with the local girls who were willing to share their favours with the local lads. This was the first time he had been able to look and to touch at his leisure. His wife was beautiful, her skin, pale and smooth, her hair, long, dark and hanging loose around her shoulders. For Margaret, too, this was a new experience; her love making with Walter had been furtive and rushed, usually outdoors or in the barn. There in the bedroom, with the evening light casting a rosy glow through the tiny window, they consummated their marriage. They may have lacked experience and knowledge but they had a deep affection for each other and their bodies knew what to do. Lying quietly afterwards, Margaret felt a mixture of relief that the hurdle was behind her and hoped that she might soon conceive. Their first day as husband and wife had been physically and emotionally charged, but as they sat at the table and shared a simple supper before nightfall, she felt certain that her marriage would be a good one and blessed the day that she had met Thomas.

Chapter 22

IT HAD BEEN a long drawn-out winter, the heavy rain had given way to colder temperatures, snow and ice and even now, at the beginning of March, the frost was keeping a tight hold of branches, puddles and ditches. Every morning, the new couple woke to ice on the inside of the windows and the little cottage was stiff with cold. As she put her foot out of the warmth of the bed, Margaret felt quickly for the rag rug, hoping to avoid the chill of the boards. As fast as her fingers would allow, she dressed, pulling on underclothes, petticoat, work dress, apron and shawl before creeping carefully down the narrow winding staircase to the kitchen. Blowing gently on the embers of yesterday's fire, she added small pieces of bark and twigs to the few sparks showing, and coaxed life back into the hearth. Within a few minutes, there were sufficient flames for her to add more sticks, and finally a few logs, as the fire took hold. She filled the heavy kettle, finding it harder now to lift it onto the trivet, before taking the pan of oatmeal which she had left to soak the previous night. With the porridge thickening on top of the stove, she sliced and buttered bread and laid it in readiness for Thomas. As the kettle filled the kitchen with its piercing whistle, she added the boiling water to the teapot at exactly the same moment that Thomas appeared in the doorway.

He didn't speak, just sat down and waited for her to pass

him a bowl of porridge. After the first few mouthfuls, he put down his spoon and looked across the room where she was standing in front of the fire, her hands pressed in to her sides, causing her swollen belly to fill her clothes.

'Are you all right? You were restless in the night.'

'Sorry, Thomas, the baby kept moving around and I couldn't settle. It's so cold, it seems so long since I felt warm.'

'Spring'll soon be here. Come and eat some breakfast. You must eat for the baby.'

Sitting down at the table, Margaret picked up her spoon and began to eat her own porridge. She ate with little enthusiasm, for these rough oats cooked with water and a mere splash of milk bore little resemblance to the creamy porridge that she had made and served over the last few years. She had never given much thought to the ways in which her diet would change on leaving her position in the big house. She had grown up with simple food, but as she had moved from one employer to the next, there had been more money, higher standards, and she had grown used to a wider variety of food, a more balanced diet and the little luxuries of life like rich cream and soft brown sugar to lift the taste of her morning porridge. Here at Tŷ'n-y-coed she did not go hungry – she ate three times a day – but there was no spare money for any luxuries. After the early months of her pregnancy – when nausea and sickness prevented her from eating – she knew that it was now important to nourish herself and her child, but the bland diet of oats, rough bread, vegetables and fat bacon did little to tempt her appetite.

On nights when the child tossed and turned inside her, squirming and wriggling as it explored the warm haven of her womb, Margaret would dream about the meals she had served at Gregynog. So real were these thoughts that she could smell and taste the huge game pies, the succulent joints of roasted beef with crisp and crunchy potatoes, rich and spicy fruit cakes, the steaming puddings made with eggs, cream and brandy. Her mouth would water and her stomach gurgle as she gorged in her mind, only to finally fall asleep before rising to another day of porridge, cold potatoes and rice pudding.

Thomas fared a little better as he still had his midday meal in the servants' hall and, although there was little in the way of luxury food now that there were no resident owners, he would still eat meat and fish and, whenever he could, he would bring home a slice of cheese, a piece of cake and on occasions, a rabbit or fish that happened to come his way.

This was her new life; a life of repetitive chores, an endless round of looking after the small cottage, tending to the chickens and their new cow, Bella. Thomas would leave at first light and not return until darkness fell, so for much of the time she was alone. On Thursdays, she would take her basket and walk across the fields until she joined the lane, and then down to the village where she would spend the small amount of housekeeping in the village shop: some tea, sugar, flour, bacon and some household supplies of soap and matches. Leaving the store, she would walk to Spring Bank and call on Thomas' mother.

Smoke would be curling from the red-brick chimney as she approached Spring Bank, a sign that the fire was lit and the oven would be hot, so there would certainly be fresh bread and maybe cake. Margaret's stomach would growl in protest against the cold morning and her lack of food. Pushing open the door, she would be met by the smell of baking, spices and butter, sugar and yeast, all mingling to make her mouth water.

'Good morning, Sarah, it's so chilly out today and how lovely and warm it feels in here. I've brought you some bacon that they had put by in the shop. Mrs Morgan says you can pay next time.'

'Come in, come close to the fire now and sit down. The kettle will boil shortly and what would you like, a slice of cake or fresh bread and dripping?'

The nausea which would have plagued her early in the day had disappeared, and she looked with longing at the fresh bread. Soon she had a plate in front of her and Sarah had spread the bread with the best of the dripping, the dark jelly from the roasted meat from the previous Sunday, and she bit into it with relish. Once her appetite was sated, she sat quietly, sipping her tea and letting the cold seep from her bones.

'Thank you, Sarah, that was beautiful. I seem to get so hungry now, and few things seem to have enough taste, somehow. I picked up some more wool this morning, I am nearly halfway through the shawl. I must make sure this baby will be warm enough out there at Tŷ'n-y-coed.'

Sarah smiled. 'I have something for you, well not for you, but for the little one, really. I had some old sheets so I took the best bits and managed to get you four nighties out of it.'

She handed over a small pile of tiny garments, and Margaret could only gasp at the delicacy of the old lady's stitching, the tiny ribbon threaded through the neck and at the end of the sleeves. Her eyes filled with tears; pregnancy was certainly having some strange effects on her body and emotions.

'They are beautiful, thank you so much. It must have taken

you hours to make these and your stitching is so neat and tiny. This will be a fortunate child to have such clothes to start life in.'

*

The hours would pass quickly with female company, sometimes one of Thomas' sisters would join them, and all too soon it would be time for Margaret to pick up her heavy basket and make the return trip. Over the last few weeks, she had felt exhausted by the time her own front door was in sight. Her boots would be weighed down with heavy clumps of mud from the fields, the bottom of her dress sodden. She longed for spring to show her face, to see flowers again, for the ground to dry up and the air to grow warm instead of the damp chill that pervaded everything around her.

On the quiet days when she sat at home alone, Margaret's mind would wander when the chores were done, and as her hands would move, rhythmically kneading dough or knitting, her head would return to the day of little Teddy's birth. She would feel the panic rise within her at the thought of coping alone. If her pains should start in the day when Thomas was at work, she would have no option but to bear the child alone. There was no neighbour close by and no way that she would be able to cross the fields in labour. Her fears would escalate and she would have to busy herself to force her mind to focus on the task in hand. As a final resort, Margaret would sing. Anyone passing this remote cottage late of an afternoon would have been blessed with a fine concert as her soprano voice would sing every song and hymn that she could recall, until finally the fears would subside and she would be calm enough to begin preparations for their evening meal and Thomas' return. Somehow, these nagging fears and thoughts would waft away like thistledown, once there was another presence in the house. She could almost believe that they found hiding places, behind the dresser, under the table, biding their time until the following afternoon when they would jump out again, catching her unawares and filling her head with terror.

The last weeks of her pregnancy passed slowly, as the day-to-day chores took longer to complete. Her body was very swollen and she felt the baby's weight pressing into her pelvis and lower back. Margaret recognised the signs, and knew that she would soon deliver her baby.

Standing at the sink on a morning in early March, she held firm for a moment or two as the pain gripped her belly and then released again. These practice contractions had been happening more frequently, and she was filled with a stream of energy. Her home was clean and the spring morning seemed to beckon to her through the sparkling windows. For the last three weeks, she had not moved from Tŷ'n-y-coed, the walk to Tregynon had seemed much too far to contemplate, and Thomas had collected their weekly supplies. With no need to carry heavy groceries, she reached for her hat and shawl and left with no thought other than to enjoy the day.

Her pace was steady as she followed the track across the fields and down to the lane. Pausing on the bridge, she watched the water rushing over the stones, as if it too were in a hurry to be somewhere else. The last mile towards her parents-in-law's house took her longer, and she became aware of a deep nagging ache low in her pelvis. Standing to catch her breath, she rubbed her lower back and smiled at the thought of her mother-in-law's tea and Welsh cakes. Step by slow step, she covered the last quarter of a mile, the red bricks and dark slate roof of Spring Bank growing ever closer. As she pushed open the gate, a sharp pain tore through her belly and, looking down, she saw a puddle forming at her feet. Her waters had broken.

'Sarah! Sarah!' she called, not wanting her father-in-law, William, to find her in this state. Bustling through the back door, drying her hands in her sacking apron, Sarah rushed towards her.

'*Wel, fy merch i*, looks like this baby is going to be born at Spring Bank. Were you not getting any pains? What made you walk all this way today?'

Leading the younger woman into the house, Sarah sat Margaret down before putting the kettle on the stove.

'There'll be plenty of time yet. We'll have a cup of tea and then I'll go and lay up Elizabeth's bed with papers and towels. It will all be all right. The men will be out of the way for hours and that's for the best. Birthing is woman's work and you've done it once, bach, so your body will remember.'

Margaret could do little but nod in relief. She would cope now that her fear of being alone was not going to be realised. As she leant back in the old wooden chair with a sigh of relief, the first serious contraction swept in to claim her, and for a minute or two she could do nothing but concentrate on riding the wave.

By the middle of the afternoon, it was over. Margaret's strong body had known exactly what to do, and with Sarah's help and encouragement, she had given birth to a daughter. A little girl, perfect in every way, nestled in her mother's arms, eyes sleepy after her first feed and the exhaustion of finally entering the world. Margaret felt that she could never thank her mother-in-law enough for her calm, quiet competence and support. Throughout, she had been a source of strength and solace. Silently, Margaret thanked the angel who had pushed her from her home that morning, ensuring that she would not be alone.

Washed and wearing one of Sarah's old cotton nightgowns, Margaret felt tired but content. She had drunk a cup of strong sweet tea and eaten a stack of Welsh cakes, warm from the griddle. For once, absolutely nothing was expected of her but to rest and look after her child. Afraid to fall asleep with the baby in her arms, Margaret carefully laid her in the drawer which Sarah had taken from the chest earlier and lined with an old pillow and sheet. Climbing back into the high feather bed, the aches in her muscles made themselves felt and it was with relief that she lay back against the pillows and let her gaze wander across the fields towards Gregynog, where Thomas would be working, still unaware that he was a father.

Chapter 23

TEN DAYS LATER, Thomas arrived to collect his wife and daughter. Sarah had refused to let them go home until she was certain that Margaret was strong enough to cope with the demands of everyday life in a remote cottage. For Margaret, it had been a time of rest such as she had never known; time to get to know this new baby, time to simply be instead of always rushing to prepare a meal, wash clothes, clean and husband the animals. She had simply lain in bed and later sat in a chair watching the views from the window, feeding and caring for the child whilst enjoying the nurturing of her mother-in-law. Sarah had encouraged her to rest, had supplied her with food and drink and conversation, had filled in the gaps in her knowledge, helping her to settle the little one into a routine. She had closed her eyes after the early afternoon feed and slept a deep refreshing slumber each day that seemed to renew her in body and spirit. It had been the best and kindest gift that she had ever received, and she would always remember it and hold the act of affection close to her heart.

The back door opened gently and Thomas' head appeared first, slowly followed by his broad shoulders and finally the whole of him. He moved cautiously into the room and came close to Margaret who was sitting by the fire.

'Is she asleep? Can I see her?' He had grown up the eldest

child of a dozen but seemed oddly nervous around his own newborn. Margaret gently placed the sleeping baby in his arms, moving away to give him space to get to know her properly. She watched as he gently took the baby's tiny hand from the confines of the shawl, stroking the dimpled fingers and then gasping in surprise as she gripped his finger.

'She's a strong little thing, the force of her grip. She gets stronger each time I see her. I had no idea.'

Looking down at them both, Margaret felt a moment of pure pleasure: here were her husband and her child. It had all been worth it. Her hand rested on Thomas' shoulder and she bent to whisper in his ear.

'Shall we tell your mother now, before we leave? She has been so kind to me, Thomas. I will never forget the way she has cared for me and the little one. I shall miss her. That basket over there is full of bread and pies and cake. I shan't need to bake for at least a week.'

Thomas nodded and called out, 'Mam, Mam can you come here for a minute?'

'What is it now, I thought you would be keen to be on your way and get these two home to Tŷ'n-y-coed.'

'We'll be off now in a minute. You can have your house back to yourselves again but me and Margaret have something to tell you before we go.'

She looked from one to the other, having no inkling of what was to come. Margaret took her workworn hand and held it tightly.

'The baby, she is to be called Sarah Jane. Sarah after you, because I could never have managed without all your help and, after all, she is your granddaughter.'

Sarah's eyes glistened with unshed tears and her lined face

showed her delight and then her sadness at having to say goodbye to the little one. The two women embraced each other closely and then Thomas handed Sarah Jane back to her mother and got to his feet in a purposeful way.

'Come on now, no time for tears. This is a happy occasion.'

He picked up the bags and boxes and loaded them onto the cart before returning for the most precious of cargos. Whilst his mother held the baby for one last *cwtch*, Margaret climbed onto the seat and reached down to take her daughter.

It was a warm Sunday afternoon as they left Spring Bank. Many of the neighbours came out to add their good wishes and farewells. Margaret sat upright, holding the precious bundle that was her daughter, never lifting a hand in farewell, lest she should drop her. She smiled and called out 'Goodbye' until the last house was passed and the horse trotted on towards home.

Little Sarah Jane had caused something to shift within Thomas. This hard-working, illiterate and rather taciturn man had discovered a small kernel of softness inside himself. He was drawn to the baby's side whenever the constraints of the day would allow, and often, in the evenings, Margaret would find him sitting next to the cradle, just resting his hand gently on the child.

Spring and summer passed in a blur of tiredness, but also contentment. As mother and baby settled into a routine, Margaret began to accept her new life and even revel in the daily chores and weekly routines. Something, too, had shifted between her and Thomas, a deepening of their affection as their love for little Sarah Jane provided them with an additional bond. Outwardly, nothing had changed – they still lived in the same small cottage, they still worked long hours for little money – but they were healthy and their daughter thrived, so they had much to be grateful for.

*

The following summer brought long, hot days and many weeks without rain. The ground was baked hard and – although her vegetable patch was crying out for a good downpour – Margaret was glad of the dry, dusty ground as she toiled up the hill towards the cottage, her arms straining to push the old pram that Thomas had repaired for Sarah Jane. The child was chuckling with delight as the solid wheels bounced and jiggled over the ruts in the soil, but for Margaret it was no laughing matter, as the pram contained not only her daughter but her week's provisions from the village shop. Her mind was racing with all the news she had heard in the village, her thoughts tumbling one after the other as she considered what impact this new owner of Gregynog might have on her family. For the past month, Thomas had been returning from work with one rumour after another about the possibility of a new family living in the house and all that would accompany this. Today, for the first time, the news was definite; the village store had been buzzing with the news that Sir James Joicey of Northumberland had bought the estate and would soon be arriving with his wife and family.

Life had been hard in Tregynon over the past few years. Many had lost their jobs, as local landowners had been struggling to stay afloat and those working at Gregynog had been harder hit than most, with many families forced to leave the area and look for work in the industrial towns of northern England or the coal mines of south Wales. Margaret had more than a passing interest as the women had chatted and gossiped: this was news that had the power to change things, to create jobs and to return some prosperity to the village. Margaret had sat with Sarah senior as she always did after shopping, and while the older woman played with her young namesake, she too had been hopeful and eager for some positive changes.

'It won't have too much effect on me and William. We're too old now, and he will only have a few more years of work in him. But for Thomas and his brothers, this could be wonderful news. Their jobs will be secure and there may be new developments, new chances.'

'I know. I can't wait to hear what he has been told today. Do you think they will put up the wages? He's not had any kind of a raise since we've been wed.'

'They may do, but you can guarantee if they do, the rents will go up as well. We'll probably not be any better off. I'll settle for knowing that the work is there and no more of my family have to leave and go away. Sally's now in service in Wrexham and John and Evan are in the cotton mills in Manchester. There was nothing for them here. Now let me make some tea. And how about some bread and dripping? I baked fresh this morning.'

As the two women had eaten their food and drunk the teapot dry, Margaret had wondered whether to share her suspicions with her mother-in-law. She had missed her monthlies and was feeling very tired each day by late afternoon. It was early days, but she felt sure that she was expecting again. Not wanting to tempt fate on a day that had already brought such exciting news, she decided to say nothing.

Reaching the cottage, she put Sarah Jane with her wooden

bricks on the rag rug, carried in her provisions and put them away. The clock on the wall seemed to tick more slowly than usual and her mind flitted from one idea to another, not able to settle for a moment, as she waited for Thomas' return. It was nearly nine by the time he walked into the kitchen; the baby had been asleep for hours and she had nearly worn a groove in the floor with her impatient pacing. Giving him no time to wash, her questions flew in quick succession.

'Is it true? Is it Sir James Joicey? When are they coming? What are his plans? Will there be new staff?'

'Hush, woman,' growled Thomas. 'I've had a long day. Let me get clean and eat and then I will tell you all I know.'

Thomas was not to be diverted from his routine and Margaret could not fail to see that he looked tired and was bound to be hungry. As he stripped to the waist at the sink and began to wash, she filled a large bowl with cawl, which had been simmering over the fire. Next to that she placed a slice of fresh bread, some salted butter and a lump of crumbly white cheese. Now that the cow had produced a calf, she was providing them with a daily milk supply and, as a result, their diet was much improved. Margaret had resurrected her dairy skills and was making their own butter and cheese.

Eventually, Thomas wiped his plate clean, drank the last of his tea and smiled across at his wife, realising how hard it must have been for her to curb her impatience.

'Now I will tell you. Scott Owen spoke to us all today. The new owner is Sir James Joicey, he is from Northumberland, he owns many coal mines and he will be coming to live here with his wife and family.'

Impatient to know more, she interrupted, 'When do they arrive? What plans do they have for the estate?'

'Before the end of the month, we were told. As to plans, the likes of us will be the last to know. You mustn't build your hopes for too much, Margaret, it could go either way. Who knows what they will do, they may bring workers form the north. Best we can hope for is that things stay the same.'

Rising to his feet he placed his bowl, plate and cup in the stone sink, before taking hold of her hand. 'Come to bed now, it will be morning before we know it.'

Moving quietly around the small room so as not to wake Sarah Jane, Margaret undressed and lay down. The room was still warm and she threw back the covers, needing only her cotton nightdress. Within minutes, Thomas was asleep, his breathing slowing after his hard work. Although her body was tired, Margaret's head refused to quieten and settle. Busy as a railway station, her thoughts kept coming and going. What of Thomas' future? Why did he have to be so pessimistic, much as Sarah had been? Perhaps life had forced them to think this way but she could see so many possibilities. Maybe he would get an opportunity to improve his prospects, maybe to earn a little more money. Her hands settled on her belly and she thought of the new life burrowing into the warm wall of her womb. Another child to care for, feed and house, would not be easy. There would be little room to breathe in Tŷ'n-y-coed with four of them. Perhaps there would be a larger cottage available somewhere on the estate? She would get Thomas to ask, and she would keep her ear to the ground whenever she was in the village. They would be off to chapel on Sunday and what better time than after the service, when everyone stood around to share news with friends and family, to ask around, to make enquiries as to what might be empty now or in the near future.

Chapter 24

IN THE SPRING of 1899, Margaret gave birth to a son, Thomas, or Tommy as he was soon known. Her labour started in the early hours of a Sunday morning and Thomas harnessed the horse and brought his mother back to Tŷ'n-y-coed. The birth was quick and uncomplicated, and by the evening he was retracing his steps to take Sarah home again. There was no room for her to stay at the cottage and so, on this occasion, Margaret had no choice but to be up and continuing with her chores within hours of giving birth. She sat in the kitchen nursing her new baby, Sarah Jane playing at her feet, and listened to the pony's feet plodding out of the yard and down across the fields. Sarah Jane was an easy child with a willing nature, but was still quite perturbed at the presence of her new brother. She leaned across to take a look at him.

'He's all red, Mam, why is he red?'

Pulling her little daughter close, Margaret answered with a smile. 'You were – red and wrinkled – and then suddenly one day you were beautiful, with pale smooth skin and then your hair started to grow in little tufts on top of your head. Tommy will get hair too, just like you did. Now, let's put him down for a sleep and get some supper ready for your Dad.'

Moving around the kitchen, collecting ingredients and dishes, Margaret felt an ache in her lower back and the muscle strain in her thighs. She was strong, still fairly young and would recover in time, but she remembered with fondness, and some longing, the wonderful days she had spent with Sarah after her daughter's birth. Life in the next few days and weeks would be far from easy.

Thomas' prediction that little would change on the estate had initially been correct, but a few weeks after the birth of his son he returned home at the end of a long and tiring day with a gleam in his eye. The children were settled upstairs and Margaret placed his food before him, knowing that she would have to be patient. As they both sat with cups of tea in front of them, he spoke.

'There was a meeting today with Sir James, Mr Scott Owen and some of the farmers. Tom Hughes from the saw mill was there and Jackson, the coach man. Sir James has a mind to improve the standard of horses we breed, to have better beasts for the hunt and the carriages, and stronger shires for working on the land and in the woods. He is going to be bringing a new wagoner and coachman, new stable lads and all of us are to have an increase in our wages. An extra £8 a year for me and Jackson, 'tis a fortune, and he's going to want some hard work and long hours for it. It will be grand to have the stables full of good animals again. We have had no stock worth a stable these last few years except when the gentry arrived for the season.'

'The extra money will be a great help Thomas, now that we have two children. Is there still no news of any larger cottages available? There is barely room to step around our bed now that we have a cradle and truckle bed in there.'

Thomas' face creased into an unfamiliar smile as he knew that the rest of his news would delight his wife. Margaret sometimes sensed that he felt he wasn't quite good enough for her and perhaps even could not forget all that she had given up to marry him. Moments like this, when he could provide something which would bring her real happiness, were few and far between.

'I'm coming to that. He'd heard about our Tommy, probably from Scott Owen, and he's offered us a smallholding – Lower Cefntwlch – out at New Mills.'

'Can we afford it, Thomas? How big is it? How far away from the village?'

Margaret's eyes shone at the thought of a larger home, a place with room for her family to grow without being on top of each other.

'It's two miles out of the village but it's an easy walk down the lane, no muddy fields to cross. There's three bedrooms, a scullery, kitchen and parlour, and – outside – a toilet. Two stables, a pigsty and we get an acre of land so we can grow vegetables, some fruit trees, maybe some oats, even. It will be hard work but we're not afraid of that.'

'When can we move? At the end of the month? Oh, Thomas it will be so good for us to have more space. And when the children are older, they can walk easily into Tregynon. The new school is all finished and there's nothing to pay now, it's free for everyone. Just think what we could have achieved if we had been able to go to school for free?'

The day of the move to Lower Cefntwlch drew closer. Margaret had packed all their belongings, apart from the bare essentials needed for their last night at Tŷ'n-y-coed. They had been happy in the little cottage, but it was definitely time to move on. She would miss the view across the fields to the woods but not the walk across those same fields every time she needed to leave the house. Since arriving at Gregynog, there had been no reason for her to head north through the village and take the road towards Llanfair Cereinion, so she had absolutely no idea what her new home, lying in that direction, would be like.

Thomas had been given a day's leave and they were up early, loading the cart with table and chairs, pots and pans, crockery and cutlery and the contents of the larder. Along with all these would travel Sarah Jane, Margaret and little Tommy and once they were settled, Thomas would return as many times as was needed. Poor Samson, the horse, would have a long and exhausting day.

The cart rolled slowly away and Margaret looked steadfastly forward as she always had in life. There was nothing to be gained from looking back. Once they reached the village, she was surprised to see how busy it was so early in the morning. It was only half past eight, and already the village shop and butcher were open and serving customers. Children walked along the edge of the lane, calling out to friends, bowling hoops and playing catch on their way to school.

'Look Sarah Jane, see the children all going to school. That's the school there, the white building with the tower. You'll be going there next year.'

The little girl looked around with interest at all the people going about their day with purpose and bustle. Usually she stayed at Spring Bank with her grandmother when Margaret did her grocery shopping, and her only visits to the centre of Tregynon were on Sundays for chapel. The village was a quiet and sedate place on Sundays and she liked this lively place and was intrigued by all the other children.

'Will I be able to play with them?' Sarah Jane asked. 'Perhaps they can come and play with Dick and Mary, Tommy is still too young to play games.'

Margaret exchanged a quick look with Thomas, before responding, 'I'm sure we will soon find you some playmates, and then when Tommy gets a bit older, he can join in as well.'

Little Sarah Jane's world had been a lonely one and she had taken to creating imaginary friends to share in her games. She had been quite content with their company but of late Margaret had noticed that the presence of these playmates had become a more permanent fixture. Only that morning, Sarah Jane had asked if there would be room in the new house for two more beds, and Margaret felt glad that in little over a year she would be off to school each day with the other children from nearby houses, making real friends and having a chance for an education uninterrupted for harvest days or to help at home. Her children would attend school whenever possible and would have every chance to make something of their lives.

Leaving the village behind, they passed between high hedges shielding fields full of ripening corn. Closer to the farmhouses were flocks of sheep and cattle grazing on wildflower meadows; the land was clearly rich and fertile. After a mile or so, they came to a bridge over the river and then into the hamlet of New Mills. A handful of houses and a red-brick chapel came swiftly into view and then Thomas was turning the cart sharply to the right and down a steep lane. He pointed to a three-storey house built into the hillside, with one wall covered in dark Welsh slate tiles to protect it from the prevailing wind and rain.

'Are we here? Is this it?'

Margaret's eyes moved quickly, scanning the exterior,

looking for signs of wear and tear and finding none. The building was in good repair and should be weatherproof. As the cart slowed to a halt, Thomas jumped down and helped Margaret down with the baby before lifting Sarah Jane high into the air and finally setting her feet on the ground.

'This is it, our new home. Come on, let's take a look. There should be a key hanging on a nail in the porch.'

The previous tenants had left to make a life in the city. They had not been country folk and had failed to make a success of the smallholding, but they had been clean and tidy. As they wandered from room to room, Margaret felt her heart lift at the prospect of so much space and such light rooms. A scullery with sink and built-in copper, a kitchen with black-leaded stove and hob – no more *cawl* cooking over an open fire – and a parlour. It was only small, with one window and a tiled fireplace, but it was a parlour. Helping Sarah Jane up the stairs, she found two good-sized bedrooms and one small one, and on the third floor, two attic rooms. She couldn't imagine they would ever have use for them. Once they had looked at everything, she set the children down to play on the kitchen floor, Tommy kicking on a blanket while his sister watched over him, and went to help unload their belongings. Nothing could dampen her optimism on such a day. The house had a welcoming atmosphere, it felt right, and she was sure that they could make a good life for their family here.

Thomas made three journeys with the cart, the final one saw him lift the henhouse complete with chickens, into the body of the cart and tie the cow to the rear, where she plodded happily behind. By the end of the day, they were all ensconced in their new homes, the chickens in a newly fenced paddock, the cow nearby in the lower field and Samson in his new stable, munching on a net of hay. Inside the house, Tommy was asleep in his cradle and Sarah Jane could not stop moving from room to room, as if the size of the house was still something that she could not wholly believe. Margaret and Thomas sat either side of the kitchen table and ate bread and cheese, too exhausted to bother with anything else. As she had unpacked, Margaret had soon come to realise how little they actually had, once their bits and pieces of furniture and belongings were spread out amongst the rooms.

Her head was full of plans: plans for the fruit and vegetables she would grow and sell; there was space for more hens so there would also be surplus eggs. She would save this money and, little by little, there would be new chairs, a rug, pictures for the walls, a tea service for Sundays and a chenille cloth for the table. She could see it all in her head so clearly as if she had made a drawing. All she had to do was work hard and save her money. She would achieve all these things. Her children would have a home to be proud of.

*

There were no grand New Year's celebrations in the Owens household but Thomas and Margaret had decided to bank up the fire and see in the New Year, for this was to be not just a new year, but a new century. As she watched the hands on the wall clock slowly make their way towards midnight, Margaret went to the dresser.

'We have some damson wine left Thomas. Shall we take a small glass tonight to wish this New Year in?'

'Yes, we should, for surely things will begin to improve now that we have Lord Joicey at the hall. He has many plans, and that can only be a good thing for the village.'

Margaret placed a small glass of the deep red wine in front of him, and together they waited for the final few minutes of the century to pass. She raised her glass to touch his, they toasted the new year and slowly slipped the rich, ruby wine, feeling the warmth in their mouths and then slowly slipping down their throats.

'The latest I heard is that there is to be an extension, a new billiard room. It will be on the front of the house and built to look as if it has always been there.'

'If he can afford luxuries like that, then surely there will be money for the estate and the farms? Who is going to build his billiard room?'

Thomas drained his wine and got to his feet. 'Not certain who will be building but Scott Owen has designed it, apparently, been busy on the plans for weeks, but it is all decided now.'

He held out his hand. 'Come on, woman, it is past the time we should be asleep. It's a working day tomorrow, New Year or not.'

Chapter 25

THE YEARS THAT followed were kind to the family. Two more daughters, Margaret – known as Peg – and Mary, who quickly became Polly, were born. The house was full and noisy, the days busy from first light to dusk. Sarah Jane went daily to school and soon Tommy would join her. Margaret had stayed firm in her belief that education was the way for her children to succeed in life and she was profoundly grateful for the chance that she had to send them all to school for no cost.

One evening in spring, Thomas looked around him and felt a quiet pride in all that they had achieved. As he put the pony away and prepared to go in for the evening, he looked at the vegetable patch, weeded and sown with seeds, listened to the ducks and chickens clucking quietly inside their henhouse, shut safely away from the foxes, and opened the door with a smile on his face. Inside, a scene of family harmony met his eyes: the younger children were playing happily on the floor and Sarah Jane was helping her mother with the preparations for their evening meal. His daughter looked up at the sound of the door and smiled.

'Are you finished, Dad? The food will soon be ready; we have made a pie today, can you smell it?'

As he crossed to the stone sink to wash his hands and face, Thomas could indeed smell the aroma of a meat pie coming from the oven. Carrots and potatoes simmered on the hob, and Margaret was laying the bone-handled cutlery on the table, fetching plates from the dresser. Within minutes, the food was served and there was silence around the kitchen table as hungry mouths set to work.

Once plates were cleared, Margaret gave each child a cup of milk and a Welsh cake before boiling the kettle and making a steaming pot of tea for her and Thomas. The children soon escaped and busied themselves again with their games, and Sarah Jane sat near the fire, her head in a book as it always was when she could escape the chores.

'How was your day?' asked Margaret.

Thomas thought for a moment, running his hands through his thick hair. 'It was good. I can't tell you how much I am enjoying looking after His Lordship's horses. We haven't had blood stock of this quality at Gregynog for years; they are wonderful animals. Tomorrow, I am to go out with him. He wants to visit some of the more outlying farms and has asked me to go with him, for fear he gets lost.'

'You had best make sure you bring him back safely to the hall, then,' laughed Margaret. 'I have some good news today, too.' She paused to make sure that he was paying her his full attention, 'I have two more customers for my eggs and butter and, at this rate, I should soon have saved enough to start putting furniture in the parlour.'

A smile creased Thomas' face, lifting his mouth at the corners and changing his whole appearance. Smiles were rare things for Thomas: life had taught him to pray for the best but always expect the worst. He knew that marrying Margaret had given him a huge advantage in life, not only someone to share the good times with but someone who worked as hard as he did to achieve better things for their children.

'Well done, I know how hard you have worked at it. You save your shillings and when you are ready for a trip to Llanfair, I'll take you down and you can choose some bits and pieces for your parlour.'

Her face lit up at the unexpected praise and support. Countrymen were not ones for compliments and flowery words but she was warmed by his genuine praise and appreciation. The warmth between them seemed to settle in the house, the fact of Thomas being content at work clearly rubbing off onto his home life, and showing in his enjoyment of Margaret's company through the long winter evenings as she busied herself with knitting and sewing garments for the children, and of the two younger children's antics.

Some new families had moved into the village and every Sunday saw both the church and Bethany Chapel with full congregations. The Temperance Hotel was doing well and Bernard Phillips, the proprietor and local butcher, had organised many concerts there in order to raise funds for a new church organ. These events were well attended by everyone, regardless of whether they supported the church or chapel. They were joyous occasions when families came from miles around to enjoy the simple pleasure of music and singing together. They brought light and laughter to a community which had been sitting under a dark cloud for too many years.

Into this quiet contentment came sad and unwelcome news, however. Thomas returned from the hall with news of the Queen's death. There had been reports in the newspapers of her declining health so it didn't come as a complete shock, but it was unwelcome, even so.

'It's that old Devil, Change, again,' declared Margaret. 'He never would leave me alone. As soon as life settles down, he has to stir it all up again. Who knows what this new King will do, what he will change?'

The Sunday service was a gloomy affair with the minister dwelling on the passing of the Queen and all that she had achieved during her long reign. People had dressed in black or grey as a mark of respect and, as they filed out after the final hymn, there was much less conversation than usual, and most headed quickly for home, keen to get out of the January weather.

Chapter 26

'SARAH JANE, COME out of the garden, you'll get your dress all dirty. Come here, now. Tommy, out from under the table! You will have a wonderful time. This is going to be a very special day.'

Taking a last look at her reflection in the small mirror, Margaret smoothed her hand over the neat bun at the back of her head. For the first time in many years she was wearing a new dress, printed soft cotton in grey and lilac, caught at the waist with a deep purple sash. She had bought the fabric at Newtown's summer fair when Thomas had driven them all in to enjoy the stalls, animals and fun fair. There hadn't been money to spare for a new hat but she had used scraps from the dress fabric and purple ribbon to trim her summer straw, so all in all she felt pleased with the way she looked.

The two older children were beside themselves with excitement at the thought of the visit to Gregynog Hall, and the novelty of the day was affecting them differently – Sarah Jane was being uncharacteristically naughty and Tommy just kept hiding away as if in trepidation of the forthcoming event. Little Peggy, at three, did not fully understand what was happening but had picked up on the general mood of anticipation and was disgruntled and clinging to her mother. Thankfully, one-year-old Polly was asleep and could easily be lifted straight in to the cart for the four-mile journey. The morning had been dull and overcast with light showers but now, at midday, the sun had come out and the skies had cleared.

'Enough, children,' barked Thomas. 'Stand by the cart, all of you, and I will lift you up.'

His early delight in his first two children had ebbed, somewhat, with the arrival of two more daughters in close succession. Thomas was now in his forties and was still working long hours at a very physical job and had little patience left at the end of his busy days. Childish squabbles and outbursts of temper would be met with a flash of his belt towards the older two and a command that the youngest pair be put to bed and out of his hearing. Margaret found it increasingly difficult to manage all her chores, four young children and maintain an orderly home and regular meals. She couldn't imagine how her mother-in-law had managed to bring up a family of twelve.

Determined on this special day that nothing would spoil the occasion, she glared at the children with a face that brooked no argument, smiled at her husband, scooped up Polly into her arms, and they were all on the cart and ready to go. Every estate worker and their family had been invited to Gregynog to celebrate the marriage of Lord Joicey's eldest son. There was to be a large tent; indeed, Thomas had been one of the men responsible for erecting it, and there was to be food and drink and entertainment. She turned her head and looked at her children sitting behind. Washed and scrubbed, hair brushed and the girls' hair curled in rags the previous night, dressed in their best, they were a sight to be proud of and, as the horse trotted along and into Tregynon, she felt a sense of pride in their little family.

Margaret felt a mix of emotions as they travelled down

the long drive. It had been just over seven years since she had walked down the same drive and out of Gregynog for the final time. Little had changed in the gardens, except that there were even more flowerbeds, the lawns and hedges were clipped and mown with absolute precision and, as they turned towards the stable block, she caught sight of a flash of the black-and-white frontage. She was eager to see more.

Helping the children down from the cart, she cast her motherly eye over them for the final time and, taking the two youngest by the hand, they set off, following the gravel paths to the wide sweeping lawns where the marquee had been set up. She had heard Thomas' talk of the new extension but his description had not prepared her for the size and grandeur of the building she was now approaching.

'All this just to play billiards!' She stared in amazement at the new wing, realising for the first time how much money had been spent recently on the old house. 'I can't believe the size of it, Thomas!'

Smiling at her disbelief, Thomas took her arm and led her onto the grass where they were soon welcomed by friends and family from the village.

The gardens were awash with people, many quite self-conscious to be here at the big house and mingling with their colleagues, many quite unrecognisable in their best clothes. Children were eager to be off and explore, especially as they could see a Punch and Judy show taking place at the edge of the garden.

'Can we go and see the puppet show, Mam, please? I'll look after the little ones. If we don't go now, we shall miss it,' pleaded Sarah Jane.

'All right, but keep hold of their hands. I don't want the girls to get lost. You look after them too, Tommy, and come straight back when it's finished. They will be serving lunch soon.'

Margaret linked her arm in Thomas' and they wandered along the front of the house, where she tried to take a look through the windows without anyone noticing.

'Look, Thomas, the old leather chairs are still there by the fireplace. I thought Lord Joicey might have brought new furniture down. They've been there since Lord Sudeley's day.'

'Well, I suppose it is a second home. Their main house is up in Durham so perhaps they don't mind having hand-me-downs,' smiled Thomas. 'They probably think it doesn't matter down here in the country, because they don't do too much entertaining here.'

'You could be right because this is a rare occasion and none of us are going to be invited into the house; that will be just for close friends and family. Oh look, they are taking the food into the marquee now. Where are the children? The butler is going to sound the gong!'

'They're on their way. Here they come, all present and correct. Right, who is hungry?'

Four hands shot up and the family moved slowly in line towards the entrance to the temporary dining hall. There were nearly three hundred people attending, so progress was slow. Margaret watched the housekeeper as she instructed her maids where to place the plates and serving dishes. She had noticed their fine new uniforms and couldn't completely suppress a fleeting thought for what might have been.

They sat alongside two of Thomas' brothers, who worked in the saw mill, and their father, William, who was still working as a carter with the horses. Margaret had been saddened to hear that Sarah, her mother-in-law, was too poorly and infirm to attend. Her old bones were riddled with arthritis and she could not have managed the journey. As the meal drew to an end, she took half of her portion of apple pie and wrapped it in a clean handkerchief.

'William, take this in your pocket and let Sarah have a taste of this fine cooking. It's a lovely pie but tell her from me that the pastry isn't as good as hers.'

Before he could reply there was movement at the far end of the tent, and Mr Scott Owen, the estate manager, called for silence. The children stopped their wriggling and fidgeting, the adults turned to give their full attention to what was to follow. Mr Scott Owen cleared his throat and began. 'Lord and Lady Joicey, it is with great pleasure that the tenants of Gregynog Estate and their families have come here today, at your kind invitation, to celebrate the marriage of your son, James, and Georgina. We would all like to congratulate the couple, wish them health and happiness, and it is my privilege to present them with a gift from the tenants.'

At this point, he handed to the young James Joicey a silver salver from the tenants and a family Bible from the estate workers. A resounding cheer went up and, after a short but appreciative speech of thanks from James Joicey, the assembled crowd were invited to return to the gardens and given instructions to enjoy the afternoon and all the entertainments that were on offer. Freed from the constraints of good behaviour, the children ran around in excitement, played hide-and-seek amongst the trees and generally revelled in the novelty of such a large space. There were sports competitions for young and old, a conjuror, and even a ventriloquist from Wolverhampton to delight the crowds. Finally, as the evening drew in, everyone gathered to listen to a selection of songs from the local male voice choir.

For Margaret, it was a day of mixed feelings. She had enjoyed the occasion, the dressing up, and had been thrilled to see Gregynog being lived in, loved and cherished as it had been when she first arrived there. Even so, as the cart finally turned in to their own humble gateway, she looked at her children – all asleep now and considerably less smart than they had been some six hours earlier – and felt a glow of satisfaction at all that she and Thomas had achieved.

'Look at them! I think we'll just carry them in and put them in their beds. I couldn't eat another bite but a cup of tea would be nice.'

Thomas was feeling mellow, having taken his fair share of the port on offer at the hall. Not normally a drinking man, he was unaccustomed to alcohol but his glass had been filled many times and even Margaret had allowed herself to sip one small glass, after which she had noticed the tensions slipping from her neck and shoulders.

'That would be good. You see to the children and I'll put Samson in the stable, milk the cow and shut up the chickens. The nights are pulling in now and the foxes will be on the look-out for a free meal again.'

With the children in their beds, a quiet evening and feeling content with their lot after such a pleasant and relaxing day, Margaret and Thomas climbed the stairs to their own room.

Chapter 27

THE SUMMER MONTHS brought an endless heat wave to Wales. Day after day, the sun rose in a clear blue sky and shone steadily on the fields of Montgomeryshire, sucking the life from the crops and absorbing the water from the rivers and streams. Early in June, the corn and oats had grown steadily, the flowers and vegetables in small gardens blossomed, but as days turned into weeks, and June moved towards August, the land became dry and parched. Grass was scorched to a crackling brown, beans withered, roses drooped and the ears of wheat shrivelled and hung their heads for want of water. Wells were drying up and every bucketful became precious.

Sitting on the bench by the back door, Margaret rested her hands on her swollen stomach. Perspiration trickled down the sides of her face and neck, and she longed to tear off her restricting clothes and step into a cool bath – a lake, a pond, a river, anywhere – to rinse away the heat and her discomfort. Easing out from her old boots her tired feet and puffy ankles, she wriggled her toes with pleasure. The baby was due any day now and she was glad to be at the end, for it had been a long and difficult pregnancy. She had suffered with nausea, headaches and generally felt unwell throughout but, as far as she could tell, the baby was thriving. It kicked and pummelled her from dawn to dusk and seemed to take a perverse delight in moving as much as possible when she tried to rest at night.

What she wouldn't give for a few hours of unbroken sleep and to feel cool again. Everyone longed for rain. The farmers were becoming desperate; they were running out of pasture for grazing and the crops would not recover if the heat continued for much longer.

She had finished the laundry and the clothes were dry within an hour of pegging out, but the ironing would have to wait until Tuesday. Each day had its regular chores and she had no surplus energy to get ahead of herself. Struggling to her feet, she waddled into the kitchen to prepare tea for the family. At eight years old, Sarah Jane was still a help to her, and after the meal the little girl soon cleared away the dishes and shooed the younger children up the stairs and to their beds. When she came back into the kitchen, she found her mother bent over a chair, a low moan escaping from her mouth.

'Is it the baby, Mam?' she asked.

As soon as she could talk again, Margaret replied, 'It is, love. Can you fetch Bethan Roberts from the Fron? She said she would come to help, and your father won't be back for an hour or so. Go now, there's a good girl, and then take care of the little ones.'

Moving slowly and carefully, Margaret made her way upstairs, stripped the bed and remade it with old towels and newspapers, resting every ten minutes to breathe through the contractions. By the time her friend and neighbour had arrived, she had shed all her clothes except for her petticoat and was on the bed, pulling on the old piece of towel tied to the head board. As the pains increased, she pulled harder and groaned from low down inside her, remembering the pain from her previous births and recalling her mother-in-law's advice to work with it and not to fight. She had benefited from the suggestion with all the other births, so she held on to the belief and tried to listen to her body.

'It shouldn't be long,' she told Bethan through the pain. 'They've all been quite quick but I've always been afraid to go through it alone. I'm glad that you're here.'

Caught by another fierce contraction, she gripped the cloth, and Bethan sponged her face and arms with cool water. Contrary to her prediction, her baby was not being born quickly at all: hour after hour passed with no respite from the pains. Margaret was becoming exhausted and Bethan began to feel worried. The sky had darkened and they had been in the bedroom for over four hours, so she hurried downstairs to Thomas. Finding him asleep in the rocking chair, she shook him awake.

'You need to fetch Dr Williams. Something is wrong and I'm worried about Margaret. Go quickly!'

She returned to the bedroom where Margaret was held in the grip of another wave of pain, her eyes were enormous and her face seemed to have shrunk around them. She was by nature brave and stoical but this was beating her and she felt overwhelmed by the way in which her body was leaving her powerless. The contractions rolled in an endless rhythm, with little time to relax or recoup before the next one took hold.

'Do you need to push?' asked Bethan, who felt sure that this baby must be ready to make an appearance by now.

'No, the pain is in my back. I've never had this before. I think something must be wrong.' She gripped Bethan's hand tightly and tears filled her eyes. 'I'm scared, Bethan. Am I going to die?'

'No, you are not. Thomas has gone for the doctor. He should

be here soon and he will know how to help. It will all be all right.'

Time and again she wiped the sweat from Margaret's body, offered her sips of cool water but was unable to do anything else to ease her torment. Finally, after what seemed an eternity, she heard the sound of the horse and cart, followed by the door opening and heavy footsteps on the stairs.

Dr Williams came into the room and, having taken one look at Margaret, sent Bethan downstairs to make hot sweet tea and boil plenty of water. Margaret had moved beyond caring about modesty and pride and endured a thorough examination with no murmur of complaint.

'Margaret, listen to me, your baby is in the breech position, this child is going to be born feet first so we must do things differently. I need you to go on all fours to deliver the baby. As soon as we relieve the pressure on your back you should feel the urge to push. Here's Bethan. Now let us help you to move, but first take some of this tea after the next pain recedes. It will help to revive you and give you the energy you need.'

The doctor was correct, and within an hour the baby was born, another daughter. The child was in good health but exhausted after such a struggle to enter the world. Margaret was asleep within minutes of being washed and changed. Dr Williams asked Bethan if she would stay for the rest of the night to watch for any complications. 'All should be well but she will need to stay in bed for a few days. Are you able to help with the other children?'

'Yes, I'll send Thomas to let my husband know. I'll make sure she's well cared for.' She turned to the window and then smiled. 'It's raining, thank goodness for that. Can you smell it in the air, doctor? Isn't it wonderful?'

He smiled back and made his way downstairs to tell Thomas that he had a new daughter and that all was well.

'Your wife will be fine but she is exhausted – mentally and physically – and will need rest and nursing for some days. Bethan has offered to help.'

'I will see to it, sir. We will all help to take care of her.'

Before opening the outer door, the doctor turned and looked at Thomas again. 'Your wife is over forty now and she works hard. I can see what a good home she has made for you and your family. There must be no more babies, Mr Owens, do you understand me? She would not survive another birth like this one.'

Before Thomas could reply, he left, closing the kitchen door behind him and walking out into the steady rain. Thomas sat in his chair, considering the full implications of the doctor's words and realising that his and Margaret's life together would have to change course.

Chapter 28

MARGARET'S RECOVERY LASTED almost as long as the pregnancy and, although little Ellen was a contented baby, it would be many weeks before she could begin to pick up the various strands of her former daily life. Sarah Jane missed many days of schooling and took on many of her mother's tasks: feeding and caring for the hens and quickly learning how to churn the butter and press it out between the two wooden pats before marking it with their own leaf-pattern mould. As each week passed, Margaret's strength returned slowly, and one by one she began to resume her chores. Firstly, taking up the cooking, followed by the weekly laundry, which had been left to slide, resulting in many grimy collars and grubby beds, and finally the cleaning, returning her home to its usual bright and shiny state, complete with fresh bedding and sweet-smelling flowers and herbs placed in jam jars on all the windowsills.

Just as Margaret was regaining full strength, Sarah Jane became ill with St Vitus' dance. Some months after suffering with a very sore throat and bad chest, she had suddenly begun to have uncontrollable muscle spasms in her hands and feet. One morning in October, she had called to her mother from her bed in the attic.

'Mam, Mam, come here, I'm frightened, look what is happening to me.'

Hurrying up the narrow stairs to her daughter's bedroom, Margaret had wondered what on earth could be wrong. As soon as she saw the movements, she recognised the illness, as her sister Anne had also had it as a young woman.

'Shush, it's just a condition and it will pass. I think you have been working too hard and will have to rest, my lovely. You mustn't be worried, we will get Dr Williams to call and he will soon tell us what must be done.'

Now it was Margaret's turn to look after her eldest daughter and the new baby. Her days were full: often she needed the help of one or more of the other children to complete the day's chores, and so they would be kept from school, despite her own values and ambitions for them. Early in the new year, she and Thomas received a letter from the schools' attendance officer, demanding to know why the children's attendance had been so poor.

'Don't worry about it Margaret, we shall reply saying that Sarah Jane had been unwell and that the others had not always been able to go because of the state of that path. You know how muddy and wet it was before Christmas. That shall be our reason.'

'It's not really true though, Thomas. Sarah Jane was ill, that is true, but the others have missed days when I just couldn't cope with all the work and delivering the eggs and butter. Some days I think they didn't want to go and I have been so tired that it was easier to keep them at home. It was my fault.'

Patting her shoulder, Thomas ignored her protests and insisted that she write to the attendance officer as he dictated. Slowly, Sarah Jane recovered and was able to help get the younger children up and ready for school each morning, but not before Thomas had been called before the judge at

Newtown court. He had dressed in his best and taken the pony and cart, determined that justice would be done and that the officials would see that his argument about the state of the path would see him in the clear. It was not to be though, and the chairman stated, 'Thomas Owens, your argument is that the state of the path prevented your children from attending, but your two youngest have made the best attendances. That goes against your argument. If the two youngest can walk the path, why cannot the eldest travel this road?'

Once the local policeman had given evidence that the path was sometimes in a poor state but that the road was always passable, this proved his downfall. Thomas was found guilty of neglect in sending his children to school and he was charged half a crown for each child. Furious at the outcome and dreading telling Margaret, Thomas left the court muttering, 'I have got to pay because the parish officials neglected to look after the path!'

It was not a happy time in the Owens household and Margaret was mortified that a report of the court case had been written up in the *Montgomeryshire Express* for all to see. From that day onwards, none of the children missed a single day of school and she stayed away from Tregynon for the next few weeks until there were new and more interesting things for the local women to gossip about.

By the spring, she was fit enough to walk again into the village and, feeling hopeful that interest in their court hearing would have passed, she set off to collect her supplies from the village shops before heading to Spring Bank to spend some time with Sarah. Her mother-in-law was now in her seventies, bent almost double with arthritis but still loved to sit and gossip over tea and Welsh cakes.

Margaret arrived on a warm day in May to find the old lady in an agitated mood quite unlike her usual calm and stoic self.

'There's too much changing, you mark my words, there's no good will come of it. Thomas called here last night and he was in a rare temper. Did he not tell you about this news from Lord Joicey?'

'No, he was tired and moody when he got home but he usually is these days, so I didn't take too much notice. What's it all about then?'

Sarah poured the tea into two cups and placed one on the table in front of Margaret, pausing to stroke Ellen's fair curls as she sat sleeping on her mother's lap. Sitting down with a heavy sigh, she spoke, 'He's worried, Margaret, worried about his job. Lord Joicey has ordered a steam wagon and a powered threshing machine for the estate. He already has one on his estate in Northumberland and now there is to be a new one here. It's coming all the way from Leeds, and according to Thomas it will be the beginning of the end for the horses. They will not need so many with this machinery taking over.'

She drew a breath and reached for the comfort of her strong sweet tea. Margaret thought for a moment, realising now why Thomas had been in such a foul mood over the last few days. She had been relieved that he heeded the doctor's advice and had made no move towards her in the bedroom, knowing only too well that she could not endure another pregnancy and birth. But, along with a lack of physical closeness had come an emotional distance. Their conversations had grown stilted and awkward, with Thomas spending his evenings in the barn, making new chairs for the children. He had become more taciturn, less patient with the little ones, his anger quick to rise and the use of his belt more frequent. As she thought of him struggling with this latest development at Gregynog, not feeling able to talk with her about it, she knew that she was partly to blame for the gulf between them. Overwhelmed with her own weakness and the demands of the children and the house, she had been too exhausted to notice his worries, too tired to reach out to him and work together to find a solution, as she had always done in the past.

'I didn't know,' she answered. 'He rarely speaks of Gregynog these days but I can see why this would worry him. They're not going to need so many horses, so he will be fearing the worst. I shall talk with him this evening.'

Sarah nodded. Taking her time, she searched for the right words. 'He's a proud man, too proud in many ways, and he's always been frightened of change. But change is coming. It's already there in the cities and bit by bit it will reach us, even here in Tregynon. Thomas needs to adapt, to move with these changes and you need to help him, Margaret. Help him to get past these fears he has.'

Later that evening when the house was quiet and all the children in their beds, Margaret took a lamp and went out to the barn. Thomas was busy chiselling a pattern into the back of a chair and didn't look up at first. Sitting down on a sack of oats, she spoke quietly.

'I had tea with your mam this afternoon. She told me about this new steam machine of Lord Joicey's. Why didn't you mention it?'

Laying down his tools, Thomas raked his fingers through his hair; the dark chestnut now speckled with grey and receding from his hairline. For the first time in many months, she looked at her husband closely and saw the lines of worry on his face. It had not been an easy year for either of them and they were both looking older, more tired and had less energy to cope with life.

'I didn't know what to say. You can't change things, it's me that has to deal with it all. It seems there could be a steam-driven threshing machine as well. Think how fast that will get through the harvest. There's no getting away from the fact that it will be a wonderful thing, but we won't need so many horses; or men, come to that.'

'Then you must be certain that you are one of the men that Gregynog does need. Someone will have to be taught how to use these machines. Why not you?'

'Me? Don't be daft, woman. What do I know of such things?'

'Oh, Thomas, listen to yourself. Is there anyone at Gregynog who knows how these machines work, except for His Lordship? He's not going to be out in the fields, is he? Perhaps you should go straight to Mr Scott Owen tomorrow and tell him how keen you are to learn. Then they will have someone who can deal with horses and machines. You have to make yourself valuable to them and then you will be secure.'

Thomas gave one of his rare smiles, tidied away his tools and together they walked back across the yard and into the house. She felt so encouraged by his acceptance of her advice that she put the kettle back on to the hob and made a fresh pot of tea. As she put two heaped spoonsfuls of sugar into Thomas' tea and stirred the steaming liquid, she pulled out a chair and beckoned him to join her at the table. Knowing that it would be down to her to initiate conversation, she picked up the paper, flicking through the first few pages, keen to avoid any topic that was too political. Her eyes lit up and she smiled suddenly.

'Thomas, listen to this! You know the rugby match last Saturday? The one against New Zealand that everyone was talking about?'

His face creased into a smile. 'We showed them, gave them a right thrashing, we did. What is the paper saying, then?'

'They're saying the team was helped by the singing. You know they sang the new song, "Hen Wlad Fy Nhadau", before the match, instead of "God Save the Prince of Wales".'

'Well, it is a better song, more rousing, like, don't you think? I can't really see why it should have made them play better, mind. Either way, we won. That's what matters, isn't it?'

Upstairs in their candle-lit bedroom there was a moment of awkwardness; their newly regained closeness would usually have been followed by love making. Margaret knew that she would have to be strong and set the boundaries. Buttoned into her calico nightdress she got into bed, turned to Thomas and kissed him softly before returning to her side of the mattress. Once the candle was extinguished, she reached for his hand, gave it a gentle squeeze and whispered, 'It will be all right, Thomas. You'll see once you've spoken to Scott Owen, it will all be fine.'

She had always been the strong and decisive one in their marriage. Thomas had followed her lead, looked to her for guidance, and on this occasion too she would be proved correct.

*

William Scott Owen was delighted that Thomas had come forward with a willingness to learn and he rightly guessed that Thomas' example would encourage others to follow. A few months after the delivery of the new machines, Thomas was the first to receive instruction in the use and maintenance of both machines. His initial nervousness was soon replaced by genuine excitement and curiosity. The end of his first day's instruction found him rushing home to explain it all to his family.

'Margaret, are you there, Sarah Jane, Tommy? Where is everyone?'

He could smell stew cooking and the table was set but the kitchen was empty; he was about to turn and go outside to search when little Peggy appeared round the door.

'Where are they all, Peg? Tell Dad where they are, there's a good girl.'

Her mouth opened, showing the gap where her first baby tooth had fallen out only days before, and she spoke in her quiet voice.

'In the stable, they're all in the stable, getting the pony ready and cleaning the brasses for Sunday.'

Picking his daughter up, he hurried outside to the stable, where he found them all just finishing off and getting ready to return to the house. The pony had been brushed, her mane and tail plaited, the bridle polished and the horse brasses gleamed. Even the cart had been washed down. He drew in his breath.

'Old Samson has never looked more handsome! It all looks wonderful, you have worked so hard; haven't they, Peg?'

Margaret looked around, surprised to hear the gentle tones in her husband's voice and the praise he was showering upon the children. He had left home in a tense state that morning, nervous and worried about the day ahead. Clearly, things had gone well; better even than she could hope, by the looks of it.

Getting up from her knees, she took Peggy from him, put her down and shooed the children before them into the house.

'You seem happy, did the day go well?'

'They are magnificent machines Margaret, and I needn't have worried about the horses because the threshing machine has to be hauled into place, and the steam engine that powers it. It can't move by itself, it just powers the drive belt for the thresher. So, we still need horses to get them into place.'

His eyes were gleaming, the new opportunity being presented to him was exciting and he hadn't shown such enthusiasm for many years. Pleased to see such a reaction, she walked by his side towards the house.

'What did you do? Where did they have the machine?'

'We hitched them up to the shires and took them up to Long Meadow on Home Farm where the corn was ready for cutting. Once the steam engine is going, the drive belt is connected to the threshing box and away they go. There's such a noise, Margaret, and the speed! I've never seen anything like it. This will be the start of such a change in farming, for there will be other machines that will come along, you mark my words. But I'll be ready for them, now.'

He swept off his dusty cap and followed her into the house, eager for a hot cup of tea and his evening meal. It had been an exhilarating day.

*

The arrival of the new machines proved to be a turning point in life for the Owens family, and the following couple of years were good ones. Thomas had proved himself to be a natural with the machinery, and so earned himself a hefty pay rise. Margaret's health improved steadily and by Ellen's third birthday, in 1908, Margaret was running her home and the poultry and dairy business, joining in events in the village, attending chapel and helping to care for Sarah senior who had become confined to her bed with a weak heart. It was a time of great sadness for all the family when the old lady died and, as they walked slowly home after the funeral service, it dawned on Margaret that she was now the oldest woman in the family. She had never thought of herself as a matriarch, but she realised that was what she had become.

Chapter 29

THE HOUSE WAS quiet, the children at school, except for Ellen who was taking a nap, and Margaret was doing her accounts. In front of her on the table was a small notepad, pages filled with her neat writing and ordered columns of figures. Money had become less of a worry since Thomas' pay increase, and Margaret continued to save from her egg and butter income. Each week, as she entered her profits from sales, she could see the amount growing and slowly she was able to buy even more new pieces of furniture for the house. At today's count, she felt sure they would have enough for a dresser for the kitchen; she had seen an old pine one the last time they had been to the second-hand store in Llanfair Caereinion. Piece by piece, they had slowly furnished the house; the parlour now contained a colourful rug in front of the hearth, two armchairs and a dark green velvet-covered sofa. All these items had been purchased second hand from George Watkins' shop and had involved much haggling over prices and regular visits with the cart to transport the precious items back across the hills. His small shop contained many hidden delights in the dark corners, as he bought and sold from many local people. There was no pawn broker closer than Newtown, so to many he was the first port of call when they needed ready cash. Margaret had found there two framed prints of scenes from Snowdonia and a dark oak sideboard which had only needed a good coat of polish and for Thomas to mend a door hinge.

She could recall now with fondness those times when she would watch her own mother looking lovingly through the door of the parlour at Cancoed. All those years ago, she had not been able to understand the look on her mother's face as she had gazed with pride at the newly polished but rarely used room and all its treasures. Now she understood; she knew exactly how much hard work and effort had gone in to acquiring each piece of furniture, each yard of curtain fabric, each china ornament. A room like this was evidence of your efforts. It was an achievement.

They had now filled the whole house, spreading up to the third floor, where young Tommy and Sarah Jane now had their rooms. Although cold in the winter, the children both enjoyed having a space to call their own, and Margaret could well recall the need to be able to close a door on her younger siblings, much as she had loved them.

One warm day in October 1906, there had been much excitement when the children returned from school. They had run into the house, all talking at once, so much so that Margaret could not make out a single word.

'Hush, hush, now. What is it? Sarah Jane, you tell me first.'

'We all had time away from our lessons this afternoon, Mam, all because of Lady Joicey. She came into school with baskets full of daffodil bulbs and small trowels and all the children and Miss Hughes and Miss Evans went around the village and we planted them. Everywhere, we've been! To the church and the chapel, along the lane to Spring Bank, down by the stream and the shop, so by the spring there will be hundreds of flowers. It was lovely, but some of the boys were naughty, they got bored and started throwing stones in the stream!'

Smiling at their pleasure and excitement Margaret turned to Tommy.

'Not you, I hope, young man, I hope you behaved yourself?'

'I did, Mam, I planted until they were all done. It was so kind of Lady Joicey, she was very friendly and she seems to like living here in Tregynon.'

'Right then, you must all be hungry after all that work. Sarah Jane, you fetch the milk from the pantry and I'll cut you all a slice of apple pie.'

Watching her children make short work of her baking, Margaret took a moment to appreciate all that she had. Sarah Jane was confident and bright, even if she was inclined to be bossy at times, a result of being the eldest she surmised. Tommy was quiet and thoughtful, always keen to know how everything worked; Peggy was a kind-hearted child, full of love for everyone, and the two youngest, Polly and Ellen, were inseparable and always content, as long as they were together. She and Thomas had survived the hard knocks and made a good life for themselves and their children. Not for the first time in her life, she felt an awareness that she was standing between two doors. To the left was the past and she knew all too well what she had already lived through. To the right was the future, for her, for Thomas and her family, and she had no idea what the everchanging world was growing to throw at them. Shaking her head from her gloomy thoughts, she began to dish up second helpings.

Chapter 30

OLD SARAH HAD certainly been right when she had warned of new directions to come. Over the next few years, many changes were seen all over the country before finally reaching the rural backwaters of Montgomeryshire. The political landscape was altering rapidly, and although the Welsh were pleased to see David Lloyd George with a prominent role in the Liberal government, that of Chancellor, his reforms, which would ultimately benefit them, also caused huge and far-reaching disruption on estates such as Gregynog. Margaret thought often of her mother-in-law's words as she sat evening after evening listening to Thomas' anger and despair.

'It's all right for you, reading from the paper about how much better life will be after this People's Budget, but where is the money to come from? How will he pay for all these pensions and sickness benefits and fairer wages? I'll tell you how. According to Scott Owen up at the hall, the money is to be raised by taxing the wealthy, not just income tax but a new land tax. That means that people like Lord Joicey will be hard hit, so what will happen then?'

She had hesitated before replying, knowing only too well how quickly his temper could flare.

'I know it must mean things will be different, but surely wealthy landowners can afford these payments. Lloyd George says they have had it all their own way for too long, that there must be change. It is time for the poor to have opportunities to prosper, even to own land themselves.'

Before she could finish he had interrupted her, standing over her with a crimson flush spreading across his cheeks.

'It will never happen, woman. There will never be equality or anything like it. The likes of you and me as landowners is a ridiculous idea. More likely, we will lose our livelihoods and end up in the workhouse. You bide my words, this may work well for those in the cities and towns, working in the mills and the factories – and good for them – but it won't change things for the better in a place like Tregynon. I can't talk about it any more, I'm off to my bed.'

He stormed from the room, slamming the door, and she could hear his heavy footsteps as he climbed the stairs. Margaret had stayed sitting in her chair and continued to read the newspaper. She knew better than to disagree and rile her husband any further – and she could understand his worries – but the Liberal principles of fairness and equality that she had been introduced to by John Jenkins, some twenty years earlier in Llanidloes, still seemed to her be worth pursuing. As she read the report of Lloyd George's latest speech delivered in Caernarfon, she could find nothing in it with which to disagree. Taxing cars and petrol, increasing income tax on the wealthy, and creating a land tax to fund an old-age pension and other benefits for the poor and vulnerable seemed an eminently sensible course of action.

She vowed to avoid the political items in the papers on future evenings when she read to Thomas, to steer away from areas of controversy and focus on safer topics such as farming and the sport.

*

Their difference of opinion in the humble kitchen at Cefntwlch had no effect on the bigger picture. No one in a position of power took heed of Thomas' angry words or Margaret's reasoned response. Lloyd George continued with his tour of Great Britain, gathering support for his proposed changes, and in 1909, after a general election, his People's Budget was passed by Parliament.

Lord Joicey had objected strongly to this budget, especially the plans for a Domesday project to value all large estates. Concerned for his financial future, he made a decision to begin selling off land from the estate, and within weeks of the Budget being passed he advertised nearly forty farms for sale. They were all from the outlying borders of the estate, but Thomas could not contain his anger at the situation or his self-righteousness at being proved correct. At the end of a long day's harvesting, he came through the door and slammed his hand onto the kitchen table, sending dishes and cutlery flying to the floor.

'I was right! I told you what would happen! Some thirty-eight farms and smallholdings to go! What will happen to all those families? It's all well and good for your precious Lloyd George to talk about sharing out the land, but who can afford to buy it? The Lewises? The Williamses? They're as poor as us! How can people like that find one hundred pounds or more? They will be bought by some other wealthy man, who will then put up the rents so that he can afford the tax. What good does that do for those farmers? None, woman! None, damn it!'

With a wave of her hand, Margaret sent the children scuttling from the kitchen; she didn't want them around Thomas while he was in such a mood.

'Sit down Thomas, I'll get your meal. You must be tired. You've had a long day.'

He sat, dropping into the chair like a sack of potatoes, all energy and vigour gone from him after his outburst. She placed a plate of hot food in front of him and turned to fill a mug with strong sweet tea.

'Eat up, now. What's done is done, there's no point in getting angry about it. There's little we can do to affect things.'

Thomas turned his attention to his meal but it wasn't enough of a distraction to quieten his frustration.

'Well, you may be able to just accept things Margaret, but I can't. There's too much change going on for ordinary folks to cope with. What will the future be like for our children? Will there be work for them at Gregynog? I don't want them having to go off to Manchester and the like to look for work. My brothers went and we never see them any more. They may as well be in America.'

Trying to keep her voice low and steady, she answered, 'We can't predict the future Thomas, not for us and not for our children. We have to live for each day and get through it the best way we can. You getting angry won't change anything except to make the children fear you. They don't understand why you are so angry. They are scared of your shouting.'

It was not only the Owens family home that was being unsettled by all the social and political forces affecting Gregynog; most of the people living in and around Tregynon either worked for or were tenants of Lord Joicey, and the unsettled mood threatened to pervade very aspect of village life. From her visits to the village shop and their weekly attendance at chapel, Margaret could tell that there was hardly a family untouched by the general air of concern and anxiety. Many of the farms sold by Lord Joicey were in fact purchased by the council and eventually re-leased back to their original tenants, but although the eventual outcome was positive, it did little to remove the ill feeling that was steadily growing in the area.

The Budget and Lord Joicey's reaction to it proved to be a catalyst for a permanent shift in the relationship between his tenants and himself. This was an awkward situation, as many tenants were also employees, and the trust between both sides had been severely damaged. Thomas had been right to be concerned, and when two years later, in 1911, Lady Joicey was taken ill and died, his fears that Lord Joicey would lose interest in the estate were realised. His Lordship was rarely to be seen at Gregynog, spending most of his time in Northumberland. As his involvement waned, he began to sell off more land in order to fund the purchase of new collieries in County Durham.

As the tensions built, many questions were asked by Thomas and other workers, but William Scott Owen seemed to know no more than they did, and no reliable answers were forthcoming. In 1913, there was suddenly news that further land and small farms would be sold by private treaty, and that the tenants would have an opportunity to purchase their farms back within a few months. Discontent was rife, farmers and workers alike began to dread each new day and the news that it would bring. Concerned about their futures, a group of men approached David Davies of Llandinam, MP for Montgomeryshire, with their worries. Just as they were growing resigned to the thought of losing their homes and livelihoods, news arrived that the sale had been cancelled, shortly followed by an announcement that the whole parcel of land had been bought by David Davies himself.

The bulletins rolled in, one hot on the heels of another, and soon the news was out that Gregynog Hall itself and the remainder of the land was to be sold. This news did little to allay the fears of all those involved, and the tension sat, coiled like a tight spring, affecting everyone in the small community. After lengthy negotiations, it was bought by a company, Gregynog Estate Limited, founded by David Davies, who was now the owner of the entire estate, much to the relief of all those living and working in Tregynon. There was still uneasiness among the workers; there was talk of further machinery being purchased and the rumours of unrest on the Continent were becoming more regular, even occasional mention of the possibility of war, none of which helped to calm the minds of the local men. Their tempers had been roused and there had been no outlet for all the suppressed feelings. Fights between the younger men became common place and the older ones continued to gripe and grumble, bemoaning their lot but never once giving credit to Lloyd George for his improvements in the care of the poor.

*

Throughout the summer of 1913, the atmosphere in Lower Cefntwlch had been uneasy. Margaret had done her best to walk a fine line of neutrality, declining to fuel Thomas' anger by disagreeing with him and only offering the most non-committal of comments to his regular diatribes. Keeping her opinions close to her chest, she had carried on with her normal routine, chickens needed feeding and eggs collecting, the cow had to be milked and the butter churned, her children required clean clothes and good food, and so she passed the daylight hours comforted by the routine tasks that busied her hands if not her head. It was the evenings that proved to be the most difficult, and try as she might to understand Thomas' anger and frustration, she began to feel afraid of his outbursts of temper. He had never raised a hand to her but the ongoing worry had turned him into a hard and bitter man, full of fury and resentment at the lack of control he had over his own life. His angry speeches would always begin in the same way: 'It's not just my work, it's our home. If this estate fails, we shall lose it all.'

His mind was on a permanent roundabout, visiting and revisiting the same questions over and over again. Margaret began to worry about his sanity as he couldn't sleep at night, tossing and turning for hours, and even when he did fall into an exhausted slumber he would continue to talk and mutter. She could make no sense of what he said, but it was clear that his mind had not released its hold on all his troubles. She did her best to keep the children away from him, but even they were aware of the change in atmosphere and had started to tiptoe around the house when Thomas was at home.

One Sunday afternoon when they had returned from chapel, followed by yet more futile conversations with friends and neighbours that did little but to whip the menfolk to even more anger, Thomas sent young Tommy to untack the pony and release him into the field. Tommy had taken off the reins and harness and led the pony to his pasture but had forgotten to return the tack to the stable.

An hour or so later when Thomas found them still draped over the fence, the laziness, as he saw it, proved to be the final straw. His anger was clearly so strong that it made the veins at his temples stand out. Turning back across the yard, he caught sight of Tommy at the stable door where he had been hanging a hay net, and lunged at the boy. Grabbing hold of his shirt collar, he shook him as if he were no bigger than a rabbit, yanked off his belt and set about the lad. His mind had gone beyond reason, his anger was totally out of proportion to the boy's forgetfulness, and it was as if Thomas was venting all of his frustration about the happenings at Gregynog on the child. Young Tommy's screams were loud and piercing, and Margaret ran from the kitchen, horrified at what she saw. With no care for herself, she flung her body between father and son, wrapping Tommy in the safety of her arms and flinching with pain as her back took the full force of her husband's belt.

'Stop it,' she screamed, 'you stop it now! You will not take out your rage and temper on your child!'

The pain seared through her back. She carried no surplus flesh, and the belt had cut between her ribs with precision but it was as nothing compared to the agony she felt on her son's behalf. His thin shirt was stuck to his back with blood and his early cries had given way to whimpers. The girls had followed her outside and stood by the door to the house, faces pale with shock and fear. Staring at Thomas with disgust and shame, Margaret picked up Tommy and carried him across to the house, where she shooed the girls in front of her. As she went through the door, she turned and called, 'You are not welcome here tonight, Thomas. You either sleep in the barn or go to your father's. I am locking the door now.'

With that, she entered the house, closed the door and the last sound Thomas heard was that of the heavy iron bolt being drawn across.

Chapter 31

Tommy's beating, although never again mentioned, caused a shift in the balance of their family life. Thomas returned the following evening in a quiet and reflective mood; he offered no apology or explanation but took up his place at the table as if nothing untoward had happened. They had heard his footsteps crossing the yard, and without a word Tommy slipped from the table and left the room. From that day on, he made sure that he was never again in his father's company unless his mother or sisters were present. Sarah Jane felt cowed and afraid when Thomas was at home and made it her responsibility to watch over her younger sisters. They had been used to his bursts of temper and the occasional strap across their legs and buttocks but what they had witnessed in the yard that day had been a shock to them all. As for Margaret, she reined in her anger, not wanting to give her husband the satisfaction of seeing her lose her temper. But her feelings of affection had totally vanished, leaving in their place a cold indifference.

Whenever Thomas was in the house, she maintained a quiet reserve and a watchful eye over the children. There was no laughter any more in the evenings, no singing and playing games around the old kitchen table. Once Thomas had been given his meal, the children would drift upstairs, preferring the icy temperatures of their bedrooms to the chill of his mood in the warm kitchen. Once they were all in their beds, Margaret would light a lamp and move into the parlour, like the children, preferring the cold to being close to him. Here she would knit and sew, read the newspaper when she had one, or her latest book, borrowed from the small library run by the vicar's wife in Tregynon.

Gazing through the window as she scrubbed at dirty clothes in the deep sink, she realised that the trees had shed almost all their leaves. The woods below them in the valley had lost the vibrant autumn colours and winter was beginning to close a tight fist around the countryside. The dark mornings and evenings brought a damp chill with them and the weather seemed to echo the mood of the country. The news from the papers became more worrying as they talked constantly of the turmoil in Europe and the creating and disbanding of various political alliances. Throughout these months, there was a constant underlying threat of war.

Margaret continued to worry about her children. They were growing up and would soon be ready to leave home, but she wanted so much for them to have good jobs, to fulfil their potential and make something of themselves. Sarah Jane, now sixteen, had already left school and started working as a kitchen maid for the Scott Owens.

The first few months had not been without their problems, as Sarah Jane grew critical of her mother's more old-fashioned approach to some of the household chores.

'Why are you still cleaning the windows with vinegar, Mam? Mrs Scott Owen says we should use hot soapy water and a chamois cloth. It gives a lovely finish.'

Before Margaret would be able to answer, Sarah Jane would take a new tack, sharing further pieces of advice and household wisdom until Margaret would wonder just how long she could keep a check on her responses. It was normal, she knew, for the young woman to become swept along on a tide of enthusiasm, but there was more than one occasion when she found herself wishing that her daughter had taken a live-in post instead of one that was close enough for her to walk in and out each day. Holding her breath and choosing her words with care, Margaret managed to survive the first few months of Sarah Jane's first job and slowly things returned to a near normal routine. Despite all this, Margaret was grateful that Mrs Scott Owen was a kind and fair employer and was providing a good training and grounding for her daughter.

The three youngest were still at school, inseparable and enjoying their lessons. They were all keen to learn, and shared Margaret's love of reading and singing. They were content still in their small world of home and school, playing outdoors whenever they could, building secret dens, but Tommy was the one who gave her sleepless nights. He had always been a quiet and studious boy, a loner who would rather work alongside her in the garden than play with his school friends. He was now fourteen and would soon be finished with school. As she went about her daily chores, Margaret's mind would drift away, jumping from one idea to another, always looking for a solution to his future. As her hands busied themselves in the comforting ritual of kneading bread dough or lifting the heavy iron and moving it over the freshly washed clothes, her brain was far away, envisaging Tommy in an office or a factory, always working in a clerical capacity, away from the drudgery of hard physical labour. None of these thoughts were shared with Thomas, for she knew only too well that his response would be curt and negative, something to the effect of a job on the estate being good enough for him, so it should be for Tommy, too. Why shouldn't he carry on the family tradition of being a carter?

There would be no discussion or debate, Thomas could see no further than the gates of Gregynog Hall and although Margaret longed for a better life for Tommy, she had already begun to accept that he would never get to leave the area and follow his own path. Determined, though, to do as much as she possibly could to give him the best of chances, she decided to seek the help of the headmaster at Tommy's school. The boy had been an able pupil and could read and write well and had a good head for numbers. Margaret felt certain that Mr Draper would have some ideas. At all costs, Tommy must not be forced into a life where he worked every day with his father. This boy was so precious to her, the more so for losing little Teddy all those years ago, although she never spoke of her first-born.

One cold, damp November afternoon, she set out from Cefntwlch to walk in to Tregynon and speak with Mr Draper at the end of the school day. There was a biting wind blowing as she stood in the playground waiting for the children to leave the building. Out came the youngest, bundled into coats and hats, shawls and scarves. They left the school, running down the lane, eager to be home and looking forward to their tea. Finally, the older children came out and she spied her daughters in the middle of a crowd of chattering girls.

'Peggy, it's too cold for you to wait around, so take Polly and Ellen and walk on home. There's milk in the pantry and bread and jam all ready for you. I won't be long. I just need to speak with Mr Draper. Where's Tommy?'

All the children seemed to have left the school and she had not seen Tommy amongst them.

'He'll be inside, Mam, helping to tidy up. He always does.'

Margaret tapped on the door and walked into the classroom where the headteacher was, and Tommy was putting books into drawers at the far end of the room. Mr Draper looked up in surprise from the pile of books he was marking but greeted her with a smile.

'Mrs Owens, what can I do for you? Were you looking for Tommy? He's so good at clearing up at the end of the day. I don't know what we shall do without him once he has left us.'

Margaret nodded, pleased to hear Tommy being praised.

'No, it was you I wanted to see, Mr Draper,' she said, lowering her voice. 'Do you have a moment to spare?'

'Of course. How can I help? Is there a problem with one of the children?'

'No, not really. It's just that Tommy will be leaving school at the end of the year and I wondered what opportunities there might be for him to learn a trade. An apprenticeship, perhaps?'

The headmaster sat back thoughtfully in his chair.

'He is a bright lad, and his written work and arithmetic are excellent. It would indeed be a shame to waste his talents. Tommy, come over here for a minute and sit down. Have you given any thought to the kind of work you might do when you leave school?'

Tommy sat behind a desk next to his mother, and felt unsure how to respond. He was unused to being asked to give his opinion, especially on such a big question. Looking at Margaret for reassurance, he spoke quietly.

'I don't want to work with horses, sir. I like our pony well enough but I wouldn't want to work with lots of horses. Or engines, I don't like the noise and the steam that comes gushing out. I should like to make things. I've made lots of toys for the girls, out of odd pieces of wood.'

'Well then, what about becoming a carpenter? They have a joinery shop now at Gregynog Hall, down at the saw mill, and I believe there are two or three carpenters there turning out gates and doors, fences and window frames, as there are always buildings needing repairs. What would you think of that, young man? You'd be well away from horses and engines in the joinery workshop.'

Margaret's face lit up and before Tommy could reply, she burst in, 'That would be wonderful, Mr Draper. Who should I speak with?'

'Leave all that with me,' replied the headmaster. 'I'll speak with Mr Scott Owen and see if there's an opening for him. Right, Tommy, I'll see you in the morning. Good day to you, Mrs Owens.'

Margaret stood, shook his hand and turned to leave, Tommy following closely behind. Once outside, they walked briskly along the lane. The skies had darkened and the air was heavy with the threat of rain. Neither spoke for a while, both busy with their thoughts.

Finally, Tommy glanced across at his mother, trying to gauge her mood, but her face was hidden by the shadows and the collar of her coat which she had turned up to defeat the wind.

'What will Tad say about all this, do you think?' His voice was quiet, his words almost blown away by the gusts of wind.

Looking at his slight frame and bowed shoulders, Margaret felt anger rise in her again to see his spirit so broken.

'He will be pleased that you have prospects of work and a chance to learn a trade. You won't earn much in the early years because they will be training you, but once you are qualified you will be secure Tommy. You won't have to work outside in all weathers and there will always be work for a carpenter. People always need tables and chairs, cots and coffins. If you work hard, your future will be a good one, and I'm sure David Davies will be an honest employer, everyone is speaking highly of him.'

After a minute to consider his mother's words and the changes that would be coming to his young life, Tommy asked, 'If I'm to be down at the saw mill, then I won't be seeing Tad at work, will I?'

'No, Tommy, as far as I know your father never visits the joinery workshop. Anyway, there will always be other people around if he should be sent there. You have nothing to worry about.'

He smiled at her, his face relaxing and Margaret felt glad that she had made the effort to find an alternative occupation for him, one that would allow him to develop his own talents and not have to withstand a constant comparison with Thomas. Grabbing his hand, she started to run.

'Come on let's catch up with the girls and get home for tea and a warm by the fire!'

Chapter 32

EARLY IN 1914, Tommy began his working life as a carpenter's apprentice. Margaret would wave him off early each morning along with Sarah Jane, the two of them walking together as far as Tregynon where they would part at the junction. Sarah would turn towards the Scott Owens' house, passing the church and the school, walking down the path to the rear door and letting herself quietly into the cold scullery to begin a long day's work. Tommy would walk on through the village, exchanging quiet greetings with anyone he met on their way to work. Taking the back drive into Gregynog he would arrive at the saw mill and, behind the large red-brick building which housed the huge saws and steam driven machinery, he would push open the heavy door of the joinery workshop. It was his responsibility to arrive first, to light the small stove and set the kettle to boil. Within half an hour, he would be joined by the two craftsmen who would teach him the skills of woodwork, carpentry and joinery.

Bill Harris was in his thirties, and Solomon Lewis considerably older, with white hair and beard and hands scarred and gnarled from a lifetime of hard work. The atmosphere in the workshop was quiet and relaxed, neither man was impatient or critical but took time to explain to Tommy what was needed. For the first time in years, Tommy could relax, and he soon realised that he had some aptitude for the work.

As his confidence grew, he began to learn rapidly and took real pleasure and satisfaction in his days. He had never been lazy and he enjoyed the rhythm of the day, from the early start to the downing of tools when the light faded and they could no longer see clearly to work. He liked to look across at the finished items and see small pieces that he had contributed to, no matter how simple, just to know that he had turned a chair leg, finished a gate post or mastered a new joint; these things gave him pleasure and made him feel proud of his efforts.

Each day at noon the men would stop to eat their food. No more meals in the servants' hall, those days had gone for all but the indoor staff. Now the men brought along a tin box prepared by their wife or mother. With chunks of crumbly cheese, crusty bread and mugs of hot black tea, they would mull over the latest news or local events, the comings and goings at Gregynog Hall.

Often the conversation would turn to Tommy's lack of a young lady. 'Now then, young Tommy,' the younger adult, Bill, said one day. 'There's to be a social at the Temperance House on Friday evening. Who will you be taking along? Young Nancy from the kitchens or perhaps there's a young lady hiding out there near Cefntwlch that we don't know about?'

Tommy's face would turn beetroot red, the colour spreading from the open neck of his cotton work shirt, painting his cheeks and finally disappearing into his hairline.

'Now, now, there's no need to be making the lad uncomfortable, Bill,' Solomon admonished. 'I'm sure he'll have a lass when he's ready. No need to rush things, young Tom. Best for you to concentrate on learning your trade before you go bothering with the girls.'

'You're right, Solomon,' Tommy replied. 'I'd best get back to practising those joints.'

Tommy returned quickly to his bench in the corner of the workroom and bent his head over his work, hoping that the blush would leave his cheeks more quickly if he concentrated on his work.

*

As summer arrived so their working day lengthened, and they took advantage of the daylight to provide new fences and gates for the estate farms as well as repairing windows and doors on the big house.

One afternoon Solomon called to Tommy, 'Pack up that bag lad, we need chisels, a plane, hammers and nails. We're needed up at the hall. Come on, now, we haven't got all day, I shall need you to come with me, this is a two-man job, and Bill has those frames to finish.'

As quickly as he could, he had everything ready, and they set out on the short walk to the hall. Tommy felt nervous as he had never been inside the house, although he had heard many times from his mother about its grandeur.

'What are we going to be doing, Solomon?' he asked as the old man puffed and panted up the sharp incline to the house.

'Let me get my breath, lad.' Solomon stood looking out over Great Wood until his breathing slowed. 'That's better, that climb seems to get steeper every year. Now then, we'll be going into the billiard room at the front of the house as there's a problem with the pocket on the billiard table. We may not be able to fix it today, but we can take a look. See what's needed, and decide then. I hope you've got clean socks on Tommy, because we'll have to take our boots off to walk through inside. You just stay quiet and let me do the talking.'

Tommy nodded before following the old man in removing his boots while they waited for the door to be opened. They were ushered in by a housemaid, through the scullery, then down a passage at the side of the kitchens and past the huge metal safe he had heard his mother speak of. The corridors seemed to go on for ever, and his eyes darted from left to right, mesmerised by the patterned wallpaper, pictures, lights, and cabinets holding an unbelievable amount of china.

The housemaid came to a halt, opened the door to the billiard room and pointed to the far end of the table. 'It's that far end where the problem is,' she said as she went out. 'I'll fetch a cloth for the floor so that you don't make a mess on the rug.'

She disappeared, and they walked to the far end of the huge billiard table with its green baize cover and six lights suspended over it. Tommy looked around him in amazement. The table was a work of art, the dark wood carved and polished, matching chairs sat around the edge of the room along with sideboards containing many decanters and glasses. The words slipped from his lips before he could restrain them.

'All this, this whole room and all this furniture, just to play billiards? All this space just for a game? It's bigger than our house!'

'Aye, lad, well that's just the way it is, the difference between them that has all this and us who don't. But we're not here to wonder why, or to feel hard done by, we're here to fix this table. Now pass me my measure and you write down on the pad what I call out. I think we'll soon have this done.'

The maid had returned with a cloth and laid it carefully over the rug, giving them a warning glare before she left.

'Wouldn't do to get on the wrong side of that one, I don't think,' said Solomon with a wink as they began the repair. In a couple of hours, the pocket was in full working order again and they packed up their tools and made their way back through the corridors to the kitchen.

The cook looked up as she heard them.

'All done? Mr Davies will be pleased, he has guests coming at the weekend. There's tea in the pot and a fresh cake made this morning. Do you and the lad have time for that?'

She had smiled at Tommy while she set to, pulling out cups and saucers and slicing the moist, dark ginger cake. Whilst Solomon chatted about folk from the estate, Tommy ate his cake and drunk his tea in silence. The vast kitchen, with its huge wooden dressers laden with china and copper pans, the black range with ovens and hot plates, the smells of meat roasting and something sweet but also spicy filling the air, the young women bustling from one task to another, were all overwhelming. It was difficult to imagine his mother working here, running the kitchen as this lady was now doing. As he picked up the last few crumbs of his cake, he turned to the cook, now busily rolling out pastry.

'Thank you. It was lovely. My mother was cook here, you know. It was a long time ago, before I was born. She's told me all about it but I never thought I would be sitting here.'

'Well I never!' Putting aside her rolling pin, the cook smiled at Tommy before asking, 'Did she cook for Lord Joicey? It must have been a wonderful place then, so many important people coming and going.'

'No, she left just before he came, but she cooked for Lord

and Lady Sudeley. Mam said it was never the same after they left.'

'Come on lad, we can't sit here all day talking of times past, we've work to do. My thanks to you for the cake and tea, a rare treat. If there's any more problems with the table, just send word down to the workshop and one of us will come again.'

When the light faded and it was time to down tools, Tommy packed up and rushed home to share with Margaret the excitement of his day. She knew that something special had happened as soon as he opened the door, his energy and excitement seemed to sweep in ahead of him, his words pouring out in a torrent of enthusiasm. She listened to him, letting the whole story come out, only interrupting occasionally to confirm a detail, to ask a question. She was so pleased with the changes in him over the last few months; so glad to see him becoming more confident. The boy was becoming a man, and the hard work was filling out his body, broadening his chest and building muscle in his arms and shoulders. Experiences such as this one today would also broaden his mind.

As she served the family their evening meal, the room was full of laughter and chatter. Ellen, who had always worshipped her big brother, was old enough now to tease him, and she had just made them all laugh as she mimicked his description of the haughty maid at the hall. The clatter of cutlery and the laughter had come to an abrupt end as Thomas had swung open the door. Knives and forks were hastily placed together on plates, and voices hushed. He stood at the sink to wash his hands while Margaret fetched his food from the oven.

'I could hear you all laughing as I came in the yard. What has made you all so happy?'

'Tommy was telling us of his visit to the hall today. He went with Solomon to repair the billiard table. It sounds as though there have been many changes since I was there.'

He sat at the table and looked around at his family. 'If you have finished, you can all get down and go and do your chores, there's plenty needs doing on a summer's evening. I need to speak with your mother.'

Without a word, they took their plates to the sink and went off to water vegetables, feed the chickens, bring in the pony and check on the sheep. Margaret felt her stomach knot as she braced herself for Thomas' news. It was a rare thing now for him to instigate a conversation with her. She said nothing but sat, straight backed as always, and waited.

Thomas took a mouthful of his pie and chewed slowly, giving it his full concentration. As his mouth emptied, he looked across at his wife and spoke.

'Germany has declared war on France today, it is only a matter of time before we will be at war. It won't affect us much here, all of us who work the land will be needed to do just that, but if it goes on they will call for all the young men, and that will mean Tommy. He will have to do his bit for the country.'

Margaret felt something deep within her begin to disintegrate; it was her sense of hope, her dreams and ambitions for her son. Her hands shook as she poured tea into their cups but she was not prepared to expose her feelings to Thomas.

'I think we've all been expecting this, ever since the Archduke was killed. Tommy is only fifteen, too young to serve, and the war will be over before he is old enough. There won't be a war lasting for years. Let's not say anything to them tonight, they were all so happy. Tomorrow will be time enough, everyone will know then. Let them rest easy in their beds for one more night.'

With that she had crossed to the sink and begun to wash the plates. As her hands moved automatically, taking one item after another into the soapy water, her mind raced through scenes of combat and slaughter and her tears fell unheeded into the warm water.

Chapter 33

ALL THE TALK of 'war being over by Christmas' proved to be false and each day brought news of more battles, more injuries, more deaths. For the people of Tregynon, life went on as before during the early months of the war; most were involved with work on the land in one way or another. Early in 1915, however, the pressure on the young men to do their bit for king and country became harder to ignore. Each week saw a few more men take the trip to Newtown and enlist in the Montgomeryshire Yeomanry.

Margaret had developed a permanent ache across her shoulders and a grumbling, gnawing sensation in the pit of her stomach. She tried hard to discount these outward signs of her inner turmoil, to keep a smile on her face and to go about her day as always, but her usual slender body became gaunt, her wrists protruded from the sleeves of her dresses, bony and blue veined. Her hair had begun to turn grey, the silver threads diminishing the former lustre of her dark brown locks. Anticipation of what might happen was eating away at her, turning her into an old woman before the eyes of her family.

Closing the door behind them as quietly as they could, Sarah Jane and Tommy left the house and fell into step as they made their way to their work places. They had had many conversations on these early morning walks about the war and what role they might play in it. They were both torn between their youthful desires to be part of this massive thing called war and their need to reassure their mother that all would be well.

The arguments had been tossed back and forth with no decisions made but, this morning, Sarah Jane turned to her brother with a serious expression.

'I've done it, Tommy. I gave in my notice yesterday and have signed up for the munitions factory. I was going to tell Mam last night but I couldn't do it. She looks so worried and worn out, but I can't just sit here in Tregynon and clean rooms for rich people, not when there is so much that needs to be done. How shall I tell her?'

Never one to rush into speaking without thinking, Tommy gave his reply due consideration, then smiled at his sister.

'You must just do it, Sarah Jane. She will be angry at first but she'll soon see the sense of it. Mam will know that we have been thinking about all this. Mam always knows everything we think and do. It will be fine. Tell her after tea tonight.'

*

Their meal was eaten, the little ones gone from the kitchen to play. As the two women carried the dirty plates across to the sink, Sarah Jane blurted her news, her words coming out in staccato fashion.

'Mam, I have given notice to Mrs Scott Owen, today. I shall leave at the end of the week. I have taken a place at the munitions factory in Connah's Quay.'

Margaret had stood like a statue, frozen, immobile, before

replying, 'How did you arrange this? Where will you live? Why do you want to do this?'

'They came to Temperance House last week, looking for girls. It's important work, the men at the Front need the ammunition. I'm not frightened!'

Before Margaret could respond, Thomas spoke from the doorway. Neither of them had heard him enter the house and now they both turned to look at him.

'I am proud of you Sarah Jane. It's good that you can see how we can all help where we can. Don't you worry about somewhere to live. My cousin Nellie is in Connah's Quay, her husband works on the docks nearby. If you write to her, she will give you a room, I'm sure. I'll find the address.'

With that, he left to search out his little notebook, in which Margaret had written down names and addresses over the years. He hadn't so much as glanced at his wife; he knew what this news would do to her but he still felt that Sarah Jane had made the right decision.

The two women looked at each other, both still holding on to dirty plates and dishes. Margaret gave a long sigh, her breath seeming to come from deep down in her body, and then put down her load on the table, removed the plates from her daughter's arms and pulled her into a close embrace, breathing in the special scent of her oldest child.

'Let's not fall out over this, I can see that your mind is made up. Whilst I shall be sad to see you go, I can still admire your courage. It can't have been easy to tell me. Now what will you be needing to take? Best go and check through your clothes to see if any mending is needed. There are two new pairs of warm stockings in my chest of drawers. Best you take them, for it will be colder there in the north and you will be standing for many hours in that job. Off you go now and start your preparations.'

For the rest of the week, Margaret kept on a brave face, making light of Sarah Jane's leaving, especially around the younger girls. While she kept busy with as many tasks as she could fit into her waking hours, inside she was cracking, breaking a little more each day like a piece of fragile porcelain subjected to a rough journey. Throughout her sleepless nights, she tried to look at the positives; the munitions girls were paid well, and Sarah Jane would be able to save. She had read reports in the papers of accidents and injuries, but felt sure that her daughter was bright and capable enough to do the job safely.

The four girls from the village left together. David Davies had provided a car to take them all to Newtown where they would catch the train to Connah's Quay. Many of the local families had turned out to wave them off; children cheered, men raised their hats and the mothers waved until their arms were exhausted. Finally, the vehicle turned the bend at the end of the village and could be seen no more, leaving them all to wander back to their work and their homes, the children being chivvied back to their lessons in the school.

Margaret had walked home slowly and returned to her chores with a dull ache nestling behind her rib cage. She wondered when she would next see her daughter, and reflected, not for the first time, on the pain of parenthood. There were many joys but nothing ever really prepared you for the pain.

With one less to care for, one less to feed, she soon settled into her routine again. Regular letters from Sarah Jane eased her concerns, and by all accounts she was working hard and had also made friends through the chapel and the factory. As her tension relaxed a little, she began to eat and sleep a little better but her mind was still troubled by the news in the papers. The war continued to grind on, month after month with little indication of an end in sight. She rarely spoke of her concerns with Thomas as they disagreed strongly on the subject.

One Saturday, she looked up from her baking to see Tommy pass the window. Immediately, she knew that something was wrong as he should still have been hard at work. Moments later, he stood before her in the kitchen. Looking at his face contorted with distress at the hurt he would cause her, she knew what he had done. The wooden spoon fell from her hand, splattering the table with flour and egg.

'Why Tommy? What have you done? You're too young to sign up. I shall go and tell them you're only sixteen.'

Grabbing hold of her arm, Tommy spoke quietly but in a voice that brooked no argument.

'No Mam, I'll soon be seventeen, it's only a few months away and they're quite definite that the youngest won't be able to serve overseas. I won't see action proper, Mam, not unless the Germans invade Britain, anyway. I have to go; so many lads from the village and the estate have signed up. I would feel like a coward if I didn't go too. I see the look on Dad's face every day when I come home. It's a look of disappointment.'

'That shouldn't worry you, son. He's not disappointed in you, but in himself. He's too old for this war and he feels angry that he couldn't contribute, be a part of it. What he doesn't understand is that you are all contributing, providing food and materials just like the coal miners. You don't have to do this, Tommy.'

'I do, Mam. I signed today. I've taken the king's shilling and we leave on Tuesday. We're to go to Norfolk, that's all I know.'

For just a moment, they held each other close and then she stepped away, picked up her wooden spoon and began to beat the cake mixture again. As she measured sugar and currants, weighed and sieved flour, beat eggs and finally placed the tin in the oven to bake, Margaret wondered how much more she and all the mothers of the country would have to bear before this war was over.

Chapter 34

JUST LIKE HIS sister before him, Tommy had left. Taking only a small bag, he had walked out of the house in the early hours of a November morning, determined to avoid an emotional farewell scene. He could not think that it would benefit anyone and he didn't want to break down in front of his mother.

As soon as she had woken, Margaret had known instantly that he had left; the note on the kitchen table had not been a surprise. Once she had read his kind and loving words to the family, she had taken the note and placed it in her old tin box, secreting it below the few pounds she had saved, her small collection of brooches and the Bible that Thomas had given her on their wedding day.

There was no alternative but to straighten her spine and face the day, to tackle the usual round of jobs, both indoors and out. And so she coped, taking each day as it came, never looking too far ahead, wary of what the future may hold. When the first letter arrived she was alone in the house, the girls at school and Thomas at work. The postman had knocked as he often did but as soon as she saw the handwriting and Norfolk postmark, she knew that the letter was from Tommy. Part of her wanted to tear open the envelope and devour the contents but the other side of her urged restraint. She felt a need to give the letter the time and attention that it deserved, so she set it down on the corner of the kitchen table and went to fill the kettle. This was a moment deserving of a fresh cup of tea, a treat she rarely indulged in between meals. With the tea brewed and poured into one of her favourite china cups, she took up a slim-bladed knife from the cutlery drawer and gently opened the envelope. The writing paper was thin, a grey washed-out colour that she imagined was handed out by the army. She opened the folds and smoothed the single sheet out carefully, before taking a sip of her drink. The moment could be delayed no longer, and with a tremble in her hands she began to read:

Dear Mam, Dad and girls,

I am writing to let you know that I am well and enjoying it here in the barracks.

We are kept very busy with much to learn. We march and parade for many hours each day and have learned how to clean and prepare our rifles, although the sergeant says we will never use them, for we are to be messengers on bicycles. I am glad that I learned to ride one when I was a lad because some of the new recruits have never had a bicycle and they are having real trouble.

We will also have to dig trenches if the Germans do head for the south coast, and it is so funny to watch some of the city boys with their shovels. You can tell that they have never had to dig anything before.

The food is good but not as good as yours, Mam, and I have made friends with a lad from Rhuabon. We get teased about our Welsh accents and get called Taffies but they all go quiet in the evenings when we sing together.

Please write back and tell me all about life at home,

Tommy

She put the letter down and drank her tea, read it and reread it, searching for any hint of homesickness or unhappiness, but there was none. She had to face the fact that, for the most part, her work was done: Tommy was a young man and had flown the nest. It was time for him to make what he would of his life and all she could do was to pray for his safe return at the end of it all.

*

As the year trickled away in Tregynon, so too did the young men, as slowly they were all sucked in to the war effort. Thomas was becoming an old man; his body was tired and his work load increased with the loss of the young and fit men from the estate. Margaret had noticed the lines on his face deepen, his hair was completely grey now and he had begun to stoop with the aches and pains in his back. He was too tired in the evenings for any conversation and would disappear to his bed as soon as the evening chores were completed. The only thing that would tempt him to sit in his chair for a while would be the arrival of a letter from either Tommy or Sarah Jane. Margaret would read them through to him as many times as he wished before he would grunt his thanks and slowly climb the stairs to their bedroom. By the time she retired each evening, he would be asleep and do no more than turn over as she got into the bed, his breathing deepening again within minutes.

Life had taken on a new rhythm. Thomas would leave for work at dawn, the girls would head off to school after breakfast and Margaret would have the day to herself. She did her best to carry on as normal, showing a cheerful face to her youngest three daughters, being a dutiful wife and caring neighbour, but in one corner of her head and heart she carried a constant prayer for Sarah Jane and Tommy. It was a simple prayer, that they would return to her unscathed. They were the underlying focus of her attention, and it were as though by thinking of them, she could in some way protect them.

Apart from the weekly visit to the village for supplies, she spent much of her time alone, and missed the company of the other women from the community as, normally, they would work together in preparation for the annual show at Gregynog Hall. They would be busy crafting and baking, working hard to produce the finest examples of fruit and vegetables, pickles and jams, but everyone was too busy coping with reduced manpower. She was pleased when Mrs Scott Owen began to organise sewing meetings for the local ladies, where they rolled bandages, made dressings and even encouraged the school children to knit socks and scarves for the service men. The double benefits of some female company and keeping busy helped her to cope with the loneliness she was feeling at home. Things would only get worse at the end of the school year, when Peggy would leave school, as her plan was to take up a live-in position on a nearby farm. She had always loved the dairy work and couldn't wait to be rid of her lessons and instead enjoy a more practical working life. Margaret tried not to think too much about the long winter evenings when Polly and Ellen would be asleep upstairs and she would have many hours to fill with her own company.

It was on these occasions that her mind would wander. Thanks to Lloyd George there would now be a pension when they reached seventy, something her parents had never seen. It would not be much, but along with her small stash of savings it would be enough to provide them with a small cottage to live in when Thomas could no longer work. She would smile to herself when she recalled all their arguments about politics but she noticed her husband rarely commented on her hero any more, other than to commend his role in guiding the government through the war.

Throughout this period, it never occurred to her that she could lose her husband. His presence – solid in its physicality and obstinate in temperament – was something she assumed was permanent. His death was never anticipated, never included on Margaret's worry list.

PART III
1915

Chapter 35

STARING BLINDLY THROUGH the window, Margaret watched the three girls struggle to peg out the clean washing for their aunt. The wind was doing its best to tug the sheets and towels from their young fingers as they grappled with the wooden pegs. She could hear their laughter as they enjoyed the battle, their shouts of satisfaction as they managed to secure each item on the clothes line. She was aware of what was happening in Lizzie's small back garden, but only in one small part of her mind. For the most part, she was grappling with her own dilemma. She needed work, a place to live, they couldn't overstay their welcome with Lizzie, they were filling the cottage with their bodies and belongings.

She turned her head as Lizzie touched her shoulder, bringing her back to the present moment, the here and now of the warm kitchen.

'I've made tea, come and sit down. You look as if you need to talk. I know you, what are you thinking, Margaret?'

Holding the warm cup in her hands for comfort, she drank slowly. Looking through eyes laced with unshed tears she spoke, almost too quietly to be heard.

'How many more times, Lizzie? How many more times do I have to pick myself up and start again? I don't know that I have the strength to build a home again, to go out to work and bring up the girls. How will I do it?'

Rubbing away her tears with the back of her hand, ashamed to be showing any signs of weakness, she reached again for her tea and drank the comforting liquid. She needed more than tea; a magic elixir which would cure all her problems was what she needed, but where would that come from?

'There's no rush,' said Lizzie. 'You can you stay as long as you need, but I did hear that the vicar, Reverend Price, was looking for someone to help in the house. Old Mrs Watson had a fall last week and she won't be going back. She must be over seventy now and it's all too much for her. Gone to live with her daughter in Llangurig. A job would be a start, and although he's new to the parish and doesn't know you, they say he's a kind man and his wife is well liked. She's always out and about, helping with the children and the sick. Why don't you take a walk down later and have a talk with him?'

So once again, Margaret found herself donning her Sunday best and heading out to look for work. As she walked down the hill towards the vicarage, she remembered the words of her old Sunday school teacher, 'God helps those who help themselves', usually followed by, 'Knock and the door will be opened'.

*

While she had set out, on that cold grey, January day, with her morale at rock bottom, Margaret returned with her prayers, to a degree, having once again been answered; her faith strengthened. Not only did she go back to Lizzie's with a new post as daily help to the vicar and his wife, she had also been given the key to the small cottage that had been home to the curate before he had received his call-up papers.

For the foreseeable future, she had work and a place to live. Later that afternoon, she and Peggy loaded the cart with their belongings, and Dolly pulled the load to their new home.

Word soon travels in small communities, and as they stood outside Glan-y-nant Chapel on their first Sunday, Margaret was soon surrounded by old faces from the past. Words of condolence for her losses, praise for her new circumstances and questions galore about her family, came tumbling one after the other, and she felt the deep pleasure that comes from being in a place where you and your family are known and accepted. She felt wrapped in a warmth and affection that had been missing for many years. As people began to drift away home to see to their dinners, she was approached by a plump and smiling woman who was not familiar to her. After introducing herself, Bella Jones asked if she would consider letting Peggy go to work for her in the dairy of their large farm. She had heard on the grapevine that the elder of the girls was looking for work. Before Margaret could begin to speak, Peggy had butted in, 'Yes please, Mrs Jones. I can go, Mam, can't I? If I am earning, then I can help out with money. Will I have to live in, Mrs Jones?'

Bella's smile had widened, 'Yes, you will, because we will need you from early morning and we're a good five miles up the valley. We'll be down in town again on market day so could pick you up on our way home if that would suit? What do you think, Mrs Owens?'

Looking at her daughter, her eyes shining with excitement at the thought of this new opportunity, Margaret knew that she had to say yes, but there was one question lurking in her mind.

'Do you have any sons, Mrs Jones? Or young men working

on your farm? Peggy is too young to go having her head turned by young lads.'

For the first time, Bella Jones looked less than happy. 'Sadly no, our son Edward went off to war and was killed on the Somme, and all our workers are much older men and all married, so you have no fears. I will watch her as if she were my own. I understand only too well how precious our children are.'

Margaret felt ashamed that her worries had caused this good woman to revisit her grief and pain, but at the same time relieved that Peggy was unlikely to fall victim in the same way she had all those years ago with Walter.

'Then it is fixed, Peggy, you have a new job. She will be ready for you on Saturday.'

As she began to walk away, Margaret hesitated and turned back to Bella Jones.

'I'm so sorry about your son. This war is a dreadful thing. We must pray that it will soon be over.'

Their all-female household managed quite well: chores were shared amongst them, meals were simple but nourishing, they made their own clothes and kept the little cottage warm with logs brought to them by Lizzie's husband, Jack. As the war dragged on, Margaret knew that, compared to many, they were fortunate. Letters continued to arrive from Sarah Jane and Tommy, and she began to believe that her children might yet return to her unscathed.

Chapter 36

TALK IN THE village seemed to switch between two subjects, the possible end to the war – with rumours rising and falling like a spring tide – and, closer to home and therefore more worrying, the rise in cases of the influenza or Spanish Flu as it was called. The disease had been rampaging through south Wales, the narrow streets and terraced houses of the mining towns were an ideal breeding ground and allowed the virus to move rapidly from one family to another with devastating effects. The newspapers were full of so called 'cures', with doctors advocating the benefits of tobacco smoke, and urgent calls for the government to supply poor families with whisky as a preventative.

Margaret's mind had been brooding on the latest news, that the illness was slowly making its way northwards through the country, and she felt real concern for her community and family. She had long taught herself to deal with fear, to look it in the eye and decide what – if anything – she could do about the situation she was facing. As she moved through the rooms of the vicarage, cleaning and polishing, her thoughts were constantly one step ahead of her: What if it came to Llanidloes? Who would catch it? What could be done to help? What if she caught the virus, or the girls?

At this point she could feel her thoughts and emotions spiralling out of control, so she made her way into the kitchen and set about making some bread. Thinking she was alone in the house, she began to voice her thoughts aloud as she pounded the dough.

'All well and good, the government telling everyone to live in well-ventilated spaces, eat good food and have healthy habits. They want to try living on a miner's wage in a poky house. All that coal dust and six children to a room. How do they manage that?' Her voice rose, anger at the unfairness of life driving her words to a crescendo.

'I couldn't agree more Mrs Owens.' The voice came suddenly from behind her, causing her to jump and scatter flour across her newly scrubbed floor. Smoothing her hands down her apron, she turned.

'I'm sorry, Reverend, I didn't know that you had come home. You take no notice of me. I was just speaking aloud.'

'No, no.' Reverend Price sat down heavily in the rocking chair next to the range. 'I have just returned from a meeting, and the influenza has reached us here in Montgomeryshire. There are cases in Newtown and Machynlleth, and according to Dr Harman, we have a family in China Street, here in Llanidloes, who are now showing symptoms. This will only be the beginning, I'm afraid.'

'What can we do to help? There must be something. Those houses in China Street are back to back, with shared toilets, so close together that this illness will go straight up the street like a flood, bringing death and suffering with it.'

The new lines – etched into her face since Thomas' death – seemed to deepen with concern. Her hands had stilled from the kneading as she spoke, but suddenly she began to pound the dough in front of her with all her pent-up fury and frustration before putting it into a bowl to rise.

Her dark eyes gleamed as she wiped her hands and stood before Reverend Price.

'We need action, action here in Llanidloes, in Glan-y-nant and all the other villages. Action before it's too late. People need help, they need good food and warm blankets, they need care for the sick and help with the children. When I worked at Gregynog Hall, both Lady Sudeley and Lady Joicey organised work parties in times of trouble. I can do it now. There are many women who will help and do the work, but we will need money for food, carbolic soap, medicine and blankets. That must be your job, Reverend. You know all the wealthy folk roundabout, so you must visit them, organise a meeting, do what you will, but the money must be found.'

Walking back to her little cottage at the end of the working day, Margaret had smiled to herself. She had not intended to speak out; she had surprised herself with her passion but the words had tumbled from her as she thought of all the families needing help. It was always the poorest who suffered the most. The flu knew no boundaries, it affected rich and poor alike; even Lloyd George was currently laid low, but the poor had no reserves with which to fight it. Not for them a warm bed, nourishing broth, nurses and convalescence. Only cramped rooms, little money and health and stamina that had already been compromised, well before the flu arrived.

The following weeks were crammed with long days and hard work. Margaret did her fair share of visiting the sick, taking blankets and food to affected families, while Polly and Ellen made endless soups and baked daily loaves of bread, all paid for by the wealthy families of the Severn Valley. She saw great courage and sadness beyond measure, when child after child from a family would succumb to the illness and die. In spite of working amongst the families, she remained immune to the disease, but the efforts she made in looking after others took their toll, leaving her thinner than ever and now with a full head of silver hair.

Slowly the number of cases dropped, and she was able to resume her usual working pattern and take some rest. The word that war was over in November of the same year brought a huge feeling of relief and freedom. There was little money to spare, but everyone pooled their resources and the doors of chapels and churches opened in celebration, while the Sunday school rooms provided a chance for all to congregate, to celebrate and – in some cases – commiserate. Whatever their unique experiences, there was no family that didn't rejoice at the end of the Great War. Once again, David Lloyd George was at the centre of things, his role as Minister for War and then Prime Minister was a huge source of pride for the Welsh, and Margaret scrabbled together the few pennies for a newspaper whenever she could, heartened by his views that such a war must never happen again.

Within weeks, word started to trickle through to waiting families, sometimes good news and sometimes bad. Those women who were fortunate to hear that husbands, sons and brothers were soon to be repatriated had often to quell their delight and pleasure when a friend or neighbour would receive a black-edged telegram, soon to be followed by a letter from a Commanding Officer, giving scant information as to the circumstances of death.

The first letter to arrive addressed to Mrs M. Owens was from Sarah Jane. She would be home within a fortnight; the men who had survived the war were returning and needed their jobs. The women were no longer required in the munitions' factories.

Even as pleasure flooded through her at the thought of having her daughter safely home again, Margaret couldn't help but wonder how she would settle to a quiet rural life after the excitement of life in Connah's Quay. Shaking her head to dispel her worries, she hurried into the kitchen to share the news with Polly and Ellen.

Plans were made for a welcome tea, and all except Peggy – who couldn't get time off work – decided to meet the Chester train in Llanidloes. Old Dolly, the pony, was getting used to a lazy life, generally only making a weekly trip to collect supplies, but while Ellen groomed her, brushing the sawdust and straw from her tail and mane, Polly took saddle soap to the reins and bridle. All dressed in their best, and with the old pony as well turned-out as she could be, they set out for the station on a cold December afternoon.

The girls and their mother stood waiting inside the red-brick building, sheltering from the north-east wind cutting through their winter coats. Margaret looked around her, thinking of that first train journey with Rhiannon, how young they had been, how full of dreams and hope that life for women would change. They still had no vote, although that would happen later that year for single women over thirty. Her mind floated back to the day she took the train to Newtown, the first time she met Thomas as he had stood with the pony and carriage, how proud she had been of her new job. Then some years later, her final train journey when she had returned to Gregynog after her wedding, a wife then, no longer with a role to play on the estate. Her new life had taken some getting used to, but the children had been the bonus. For the first time in many months, she was able to think of Thomas with affection, and to remember those early years as a mother with real pleasure. The station had been a spectator at some of the most memorable moments of her life.

Polly shook her arm. 'It's coming, Mam, I see the train! I wonder if we'll recognise Sarah Jane? She may have changed, it's been over three years. Do you think she'll recognise me, Mam?'

'Shush, child, too many questions. Of course she will know you. Now, look, people are beginning to get off. Can you see her?'

Margaret scanned the crowd, her eyes searching for her tall dark-haired daughter. Suddenly she saw her and moved forward, calling her name.

'Sarah Jane, Sarah Jane, over here.'

Sarah Jane heard her mother's voice, waved and reached behind her for her bag. The young girl who had left the farm at Tregynog was returning as a woman. Still tall, still slim, but dressed in the shorter dress length of the day, her shapely stockinged ankles were being closely admired by the soldier helping to lift her bag from the train. Giving him a smile of thanks, she gathered speed before dropping the bag again, throwing her arms around her mother and being engulfed by her sisters.

Finally, the four disentangled themselves, and made their way out of the station. Pulling off her woollen gloves, Sarah Jane reached out a hand to Dolly, and as the old pony recognised her, she snickered with pleasure, pushing her nose into Sarah Jane's side.

'She still remembers you! I've been telling her that you were coming home, haven't I, Mam?'

Now fifteen and longing to see her sister again, Polly was beside herself with excitement, hopping from one foot to the other.

Margaret climbed into the front of the cart, took up the reins and called, 'Come on, it's too cold to linger here. Let's get home. You two, in the back. Put your bag under your feet, Sarah Jane, and sit here next to me.'

They made their way down Broad Street and past the market hall, with the two youngest pointing out every building of note, any person they recognised. Sarah Jane listened with one ear and replied automatically while her mind grappled with the shock of her mother's appearance. She had not been prepared for such a change and it was clear that the last three years had not been kind to her: grief, worry, hard work and lack of money had robbed Margaret of her looks. The only things that hadn't changed were her voice and her personality. As they crossed the bridge and headed out of town, she commented on the sight of so many men on the street corners.

'Why are they just standing about, Mam? Are they ill or wounded?'

'Some are, some very badly, some have breathing problems because of the gas. Each time I come to town, there seems to be more of them. Every train has soldiers on it, you could see that today. It's wonderful that they have returned safely, but what is there for them now? Didn't you see men like this in Connah's Quay?'

'Yes, but not as many just standing on the street. Are there no jobs? What about the wounded, what will happen to them?'

'Not a lot here in Llanidloes. In Newtown, David Davies, from Gregynog, he's MP now and I read in the *Express* that he's opened a meeting place and a training centre to teach the men new skills. But here? As far as I know, there's nothing, only farming and the Van mine, and most of them don't look fit enough for either of those.'

Margaret could see on her eldest daughter's face the anger at Sarah's own situation – having to quit her job for returning soldiers – dissipating, to be replaced by empathy for these men, hanging around sadly on street corners.

Chapter 37

PEGGY HAD COME home for the day on Sunday, bringing with her butter, cream and eggs from the farm, and one of Bella Jones' meat and potato pies. She and Sarah Jane had been so pleased to be reunited, and the little cottage was full of chatter and laughter from the moment they returned from chapel. Margaret peeled potatoes and chopped cabbage, laid the old table for five and then sat, eating little but listening and watching her girls all together again. Their words and laughter were like a healing balm, and for the first time in many weeks she felt the muscles in her neck and shoulders begin to relax and lose their stiffness.

When Peggy rose to get her coat, Sarah Jane offered to walk halfway with her, and as they closed the door behind them, Margaret felt the energy in the room drop a notch in the warm kitchen. Polly and Ellen set to clearing away the remains of the meal, clattering crockery and pans as they restored the cottage to order. Margaret's eyes felt heavy, the girls' voices seemed to be coming from farther away and she slipped into a light sleep.

Outside the sky was darkening, and Sarah Jane tucked her arm into Peggy's, enjoying having her sister close again.

'Are you liking your job at the farm? Do they treat you well?'

'I love it. They are good to me. I have plenty to eat, as you can see!' She pointed to the front of her coat where the buttons were beginning to show signs of strain. Peggy had always liked her food and found it difficult to say no when anything tasty was on offer.

'I have my own little room and I think Mrs Jones is glad to have another woman about the place. It must have been lonely for her with only the men for company. We all sit together in the evenings and sometimes Mr Jones plays the harmonium and we have a sing-song. Sometimes we sew or read, because they have lots of books. It is a good job. I was lucky to get it. What about you? What are you going to do? There aren't many jobs around at the moment.'

'No, I know. I shall have to get something, bring some money in, because Mam needs to be working fewer hours. Have you seen how tired she is? And she doesn't eat much. Did you notice how she pushed her food around? Do you think she's ill?'

'No, I don't think it's an illness of her body. I think she's worn out with worry. She works too hard, worries too much and frets about Tommy. I think she'll be better when he gets home. Why don't you try at the Trewythen Arms for work? They always seem to be busy when we are in town; they may have something?'

Their conversation turned to old friends in Tregynon, to a dress that Peggy was making and the social to be held at the schoolroom in a few weeks.

'I want the dress finished for the social,' said Peggy, 'I want to look my best, you never know who may be there?'

Laughing and teasing each other, they continued on to the bend in the road. Holding each other close for a few minutes, they stepped back and went their separate ways, each one disappearing into the darkness of evening. As Sarah Jane trudged back down the valley, eager to be back in the warm kitchen with a cup of hot tea, she made up her mind that she would definitely call at the Trewythen on the next visit to town.

*

The week that Sarah Jane started her new job as a chamber maid in the hotel, another letter arrived for Margaret, this time with news that Tommy was to be coming home. There was no actual date for his arrival but he expected it to be within the next ten days or so. Margaret's first thoughts were full of delight and relief, but they were soon followed by more practical concerns. Where would he sleep? They only had two bedrooms; Polly and Ellen shared the smaller of the two and now Sarah Jane was sleeping with her in the other room. The only solution was to put up a folding bed in the cold and rather bleak little parlour, which they rarely used. She was able to borrow a bed and some blankets from Mrs Price, and the girls soon had it made up. The room faced north and was always cold, so each evening she lit a fire, not wanting him to arrive unexpectedly and find a cold room.

Impatience and excitement were making her jumpy and irritable, and when finally there was a knock at the door, she ran to answer it. Seeing her son standing there, Margaret promptly burst into tears.

'Oh Tommy, I thought I should never see you again? What a silly woman I am, come in, come in out of the cold.'

Tommy had grown taller, filled out and was now a man. Carrying his heavy kit bag with ease, he lowered his head and entered the tiny cottage. Holding out his arms to his mother, she rested her head on his shoulder, savouring the moment, the feel of him in her arms again. Her heart felt full to have her prayers answered, but never one to wallow in sentimentality she soon recovered herself.

'Take off that coat, and come here by the fire. I'll put the kettle on and make tea. Are you hungry? When did you leave?'

Tommy smiled. 'I left early this morning Mam, and I've had nothing all day but a cup of tea and a bun at Shrewsbury station. There was a table all set up on the platform with ladies serving drinks and cakes to the soldiers. They were rushed off their feet, there's so many moving around and heading home. I could do with something, a bit of bread and cheese, perhaps?'

Within minutes, he was attacking a plate laden with crusty bread, strong cheese and slices of raw onion. His mug was filled and then refilled with strong tea. While he ate, Margaret's eyes feasted on him, enjoying these quiet moments before the girls would come home and take up their brother's attention. Just for now, he was home, he was safe and he was all hers. There would be time for talking, later.

Chapter 38

THE FAMILY SETTLED into a new routine, and Tommy would set off each day to look for work, initially in the local area in and around Llanidloes. But, as he failed to find any, he took the train as far as Newtown and Rhayader. He was not alone in his searching, as many young men were in the same position, and day after day he returned disappointed. The small cottage was beginning to feel cramped and Tommy was becoming bored and dispirited. He had grown used to the open countryside and sweeping coastline of Norfolk; he had enjoyed having full days and the companionship of his fellow soldiers. In comparison, life at home felt tedious and increasingly lacking in purpose. Much as he loved his mother and sisters, being in such close quarters with so many women taxed his patience, and he longed for the company of men, hard work and a satisfying pint of beer at the end of the day. His mood grew darker and his frustration at the situation would on occasions cause him to lose his temper over the slightest thing.

Returning one afternoon – drenched through, cold and tired – he slumped into the chair by the side of the hearth. Without thought or planning, the words tumbled from him as he watched his mother brewing the tea.

'Mam, I shall have to leave. I can't stay here, I'm a burden to you and I need to be working. I hate to ask, but can you give me the price of a train ticket to the south? There's bound to be more work down there. The mines need carpenters to make the pit props. I shall do better down there.'

With a heavy heart she answered, 'Yes, I can give you the money. I'm sorry there's no work here, I know how hard you've tried. Where will you go? Where will you stay? We don't know anyone down there.'

'I'll be fine. Once I have work, I'll soon find some lodgings. I have to do something. I can't sit around here for the rest of my days like all the other victims of the war. At least I still have my health and strength.'

Margaret knew that there was no point in arguing with him. She could understand his feelings and, whilst she loved having him near her again, she could see that it was no life for a young man. Within a day, he had gone, and she took his army photograph and hung it on the chimney breast. He had looked so smart in his uniform and she would glance at the picture whenever she came back into the room.

Within a week, a postcard arrived with a picture of Swansea Bay, but all he had written was, 'All is well, Mam. I'll send an address soon, Tommy.' The days passed and turned into weeks, the weeks into months but no card or letter arrived.

Sarah Jane took Polly and Ellen to one side when their mother was in the garden. 'It's best you don't ask any more about Tommy; she gets so upset whenever his name is mentioned that I think we should stay quiet. There's no way of finding out where he is or what's happened, so we just have to pretend that we're not worried. That way, she won't have to think about him all the time.'

'It's not that simple,' said Polly. 'Haven't you noticed how often she looks at his picture? She's pretending not to worry for our sakes but she thinks of him all the time.'

'Well, I think he's plain selfish,' pouted Ellen crossly. 'How much effort does it take to send a card? He must know that she would worry.'

Sarah Jane looked at the two younger girls and realised how grown up they had become over the past year.

'Look, we don't know what has happened to him. He may have caught the Spanish Flu and died. He might have got hurt down a mine or been in an accident. We just don't know.'

'I know that,' said Ellen, 'but he might have earned enough money for a ticket to America or Canada, it's been months now. You read the paper. You see how many men are heading off, looking for a new life. All he had to do was tell us. I shan't have anything to do with him if he comes back. He was always her favourite, always got to do what he wanted. He can stay away for ever, for all I care.'

'Me too,' said Polly. 'Look at all the upset he's caused. Poor Mam, she's looking so old these days. You're right, let's try and forget about him.'

The girls made a determined effort not to mention Tommy in the months to come, and although Margaret noticed she made no comment. She continued to worry, to pray for his safety, clinging to the small chance that he was still alive and well, and would one day return.

Slowly, the walls of the little cottage seemed to expand again, as Sarah Jane too left home for the second time. For some months she had been walking out with David Davies, another young soldier returned from the war. They had met one evening as she was leaving work in town, and after that he had made a point of waiting outside the hotel as often as he could and offering to walk her home. He came from a farming family near Llangurig, and for the time being at least he had work on a local farm. David soon became a regular visitor at the cottage, sharing meals and accompanying the little family to chapel services.

One evening, Margaret and Sarah Jane were sitting reading by the fire.

'Mam, me and Dai, we're going to be married. Are you pleased about that?'

Margaret smiled and patted her daughter's hand. 'I guessed it would be happening. He's a good man and you seem content with him. When are you thinking of having a wedding?'

Sarah Jane shifted in her seat, looking uncomfortable, grasped for the right words and stammered. 'Soon, Mam, in the next six weeks, I think. We'll talk to the minister after chapel on Sunday.'

'Ah. I see,' said Margaret. 'You're sure you're expecting?'

Nodding, Sarah Jane blushed. 'I'm sorry, Mam.'

'Don't worry, you're not the first nor the last. It will be fine and he's standing by you and that's what matters.'

Knowing that history was about to repeat itself again brought back all the memories of her time at Tŷ Uchaf and how awful it had been to be shunned by the Williams family and sent home in disgrace. Taking a deep breath, she knew that there would never be a better time to share this story with her daughter.

'Put another log on that fire, Sarah Jane; there is something I should tell you.'

Chapter 39

A NEW DECADE brought with it a new rhythm to life. Ellen and Polly both had jobs now, Ellen in the laundry and Polly in Jones', the drapers' shop, and with more money coming in, Margaret was at last able to cut her working hours. Now she headed to the vicarage just for the morning, primarily cooking for the Reverend and his family while a young girl took on the heavy work.

Nineteen twenty saw the birth of her first grandchild, a girl, also called Margaret but known from day one as Peg. The child brought joy and affection, warmth and delight back into Margaret's life and she fitted in as many visits to Sarah Jane's little cottage as she could, feeling her spirits lift as she spent time with her daughter and granddaughter. Her little namesake had a sunny disposition, and one afternoon, as they were playing together with a set of building bricks, her baby chatter suddenly quietened. As she handed her grandmother a brick in her chubby little hand, she said, 'Gally'. The little girl's mispronunciation, of Granny to Gally, became Margaret's new name, a term of endearment used by all the family, and the grandchildren who later followed. A new name for a new time in her life seemed fitting, and she enjoyed her new persona.

Her regular evenings with the papers brought continued news of both Montgomeryshire and further afield. There had been ongoing changes at Gregynog, with the total contents of the hall being sold in a one-day auction. As she read the long list of items that had been disposed of, she sat by her small fire, recalling her days in the big house. It seemed so long ago in one way, but in another, still so vivid: the dressers and sideboards, art work and china, beds and wardrobes that were listed had all been under her care at one time or another, and now they were being sold off with little thought for their history. It pained her to think of the contents being separated, disappearing into the homes of the county's wealthiest landowners so that they could boast of their new acquisitions and their association with Gregynog Hall.

Just a few weeks later came the news that David Davies had sold the hall and three hundred acres of land to his sisters, Gwendoline and Margaret, who intended making Gregynog into a centre for Welsh music, arts and crafts. With two spinster sisters, there was little chance of a new dynasty to retain the estate as a family concern. Gally laid down her paper, poured a fresh cup of tea and muttered, 'Well we're not done yet, Gregynog Hall and I: we might be older and a bit creaky but both me and that old house, we're still here, still going strong.'

Sarah Jane was now expecting again, so each afternoon Gally would head over to her daughter's home and take care of young Peg for a few hours while her mother took a nap. Each week, her younger daughters would hand over a share of their earnings, and for the first time since moving back to Llanidloes there was money for a few non-essentials. They attended an occasional concert in one of the large chapels, had even visited the new cinema in Great Oak Street to watch the black-and-white silent films. A newspaper was no longer a once-a-week luxury but something to be purchased on every trip into town. The highlight of the week was Tuesday, when the *Montgomeryshire Express* was published and Gally never missed a trip to the newsagent's for her copy.

On a cold January evening in 1921, she picked up the paper to see – on the first page – the announcement of William Scott Owen's death. It had been unexpected, without warning and so came as a huge shock to both his family and the community in and around Tregynon. Gally's thoughts returned to the day he had arrived at Cefntwlch and presented her with her marching orders. It had been the last time she had ever spoken to him, and – although it was understandable that she had been angry at the time – it was not his fault that she had lost her job and house on Thomas' death, and she felt regret that there had never been an opportunity to express how she felt. Now it was too late. Her mind wandered back through the years, and she thought again of all the help he had given her when she first went to Gregynog Hall, his support for her and Thomas in their marriage and in later years, his backing for Thomas and encouragement for him to learn new skills. He had been a good man, and she mourned his passing. Gregynog estate would not be the same without him.

Her eyes closed and she slipped into a dream-like state. Her mind roamed back over the years: she had noticed this happening much more in recent years, and, in many ways, the past now seemed to be more real and vivid than the previous day or week. How pleased and proud she had been when she had first been given the job at Gregynog Hall; perhaps, too proud. How she had loved the fitted black dress and the smart white apron and cap she had worn when Lord Sudeley was owner! How everything had changed when she and Thomas had wed. They had been poor, it had felt like being in the

Snakes & Ladders game the children had later played; she had taken a tumble down that snake at speed and not really been prepared for the hardships of their life together in the early years.

A log slipped in the fireplace and the noise roused her from her reverie. The room had grown colder and her bones were stiff, her neck aching from sitting awkwardly. She looked at the clock, realising that the girls would be home soon and wanting the warmth of a good fire and food, so she stretched her limbs, rattled the fire and added more wood before starting to prepare a meal. The familiar actions calmed her mind and she thought – not for the first time – about the futility of looking back and, even more so, of trying to guess what the future might hold.

Just a fortnight later she was shocked, when entering the newsagent's to buy her paper, to find many more people in there than was usual, and a buzz of chatter. There had been rumours, in the previous few days, of a train crash at Abermule and finally the details were there in print for everyone to see. The headlines were horrifying, and Gally walked as quickly as she could to reach Sarah Jane's cottage. She sat down heavily to catch her breath and Peg quickly climbed on to her lap.

'Gally play, Gally play with Peg.'

The little girl's voice caught her attention and she scooped up the bricks, starting to build a tower on the table. Delighted Peg clapped her hands together but, as her grandmother placed the final brick on top of the tower, she chortled with laughter and knocked it down again.

'More Gally, do more again.'

Gally's face creased with smiles but she gently placed the tot on the floor with her toys.

'In a minute, cariad. I need to talk to Mam first. You be patient.'

Reaching into her bag she pulled out the newspaper and opened it at the front page.

'It's terrible news, Sarah Jane, no one seems to know what caused the accident. How could two trains be heading for each other on a single track? So many injuries and deaths.'

Sarah Jane passed her mother a cup of tea. 'Do they know how many? Everyone seems to know someone who was involved in some way. Dai was full of it last night when he got home.'

Gally scanned the article for numbers. 'Seventeen have died, many were lucky to escape alive with only minor injuries.' She took a drink of her tea before turning back to the paper. 'Oh no. One of the dead was Gwendolyn Scott Owen. She had been home for her father's funeral. Oh, how sad, how very, very sad.'

Gally felt as though she could not escape from her past. The news from Gregynog and the Scott Owen family seemed to drag her back in time. She had tried so hard to banish the sadness and anger she had felt after Thomas' death, but the latest developments were hard to take, along with her continuing worries about Tommy. There was an empty space in her heart, a vacuum where there should have been a son. She mentioned him in her prayers every night and looked for a letter every day. Just because she didn't talk about him all the time didn't mean that she didn't feel his loss deeply. Life had taught her to keep her fears and worries to herself, for talking about them wouldn't change a thing. Her anxiety was a constant emotion, eating away, little by little, at her new-found contentment.

Each evening before she went up to bed Gally had taken to opening the curtains slightly and leaving a lighted candle in the window. 'Just in case,' she would say to herself. 'Just in case it's tonight he comes home. The path outside is slippery and it will help him to find his way in the dark.'

There is always balance in life, however, and in September a second granddaughter, Marie, was born. Two years later, a first grandson, David, was followed by two more: Roland and Richard. These children of Sarah Jane's helped to heal the wounds of loss and despair, and gradually she bloomed in the warmth of their simple love and laughter. Their company became a balm to all that she had suffered, and their simple pleasures and joy in life rekindled her soft smiles and sweet singing.

As the children grew up, life in mid Wales – as in many rural parts of the country – grew more difficult. There were fewer jobs and less money as the reality of the post-war depression began to spread from the major cities and affect the countryside and small market towns. Eventually, Sarah Jane's husband Dai felt that he had no option other than to leave his family and head to the Valleys of south Wales in search of work.

Gally felt a mix of emotions, sadness and sympathy for her daughter at having to manage her family without the support of her husband, but also a flicker of hope that he might just hear something about Tommy. A few days before he left, she managed to corner him in the garden. 'Dai, come here for a minute. I want to speak with you.'

Pulling him closer so that she would not have to raise her voice – for she was afraid that Sarah Jane might overhear them – she whispered urgently, 'I know it's unlikely, but you will keep your ears and eyes open for any news of Tommy, won't you? He may have gone to the mines and someone may just pick up when they hear you are from Llanidloes too.'

Caught in the middle of the two women – for Dai had heard many times of his wife's frustration with the disappearance of her brother – but feeling sorry for the old lady who was such a support to them all, he looked around before answering. There was no one else in sight so he rested his arm lightly on her shoulders as he spoke. 'Of course, Gally, you know that I will let you know, as soon as I can, if there is any news, good or bad. I think now you just need to know, don't you?'

'That's good of you, there's no need to mention it to anyone else, no need to get anyone's temper up, is there?' She smiled at him as he walked back towards the cottage. 'You look after yourself down there, and take care in those mines. We need you to come back when things improve; those boys need a father around.'

Chapter 40

IT WAS LATE in the afternoon that Gally ran as fast as her aging legs would carry her, down the cinder path to Sarah Jane's cottage. In her hand was the latest edition of the *Montgomeryshire Express*. She was breathing hard by the time she entered the kitchen and dropped into a chair to regain her composure. Roly and Dickie, the youngest two, were busy playing on the floor with an old saucepan and a collection of wooden dolly pegs. She watched them in silence for a few minutes and nodded in response to the question, 'Cup of tea, Mam?'

As the cup was passed to her, she opened the paper to the advertisements, pointing to the properties for rent at the bottom of the page. 'Look here, out at Nantyrhebog, two cottages adjoining, right by the river. They only cost a little more than we are both paying now. We could be next door to each other and I could have one of the children to sleep with me. It would give you so much more room. You're so squashed up here.'

'Wait a minute, Mam, wait a minute. You're rushing me. What cottages? Let me see.'

Sarah Jane took the page and read through the advertisement carefully. 'It's further out of town, Mam, for the children. What about school?'

'They can go to school at Old Hall; there's a good little

school there and you won't be having to worry about them walking back from town. You can't carry on like this on your own any longer. Have you heard from Dai? What is happening with you both?'

Her daughter's eyes filled with tears and she struggled to control her emotions. She was worn out with trying to run the home, look after the children and take in any washing and ironing she could find, to help make ends meet.

'He won't be coming back, Mam. Each time he came home to visit, things just got worse. He doesn't want to be around people. He loves the children. I can see it in his eyes, but their noise and chatter make him so jumpy and angry. He won't talk about it, but I think it must be something to do with the war, something caused by the fighting. He's happier down there in south Wales, working with the men and living in lodgings. He sends me money every few weeks but there's no hope of a life together again.'

Gally paused, disturbed by this news, and full of concern for her daughter, but stubborn and practical as ever.

'In that case, this is the answer! I can help out, as can your sisters. When these two monkeys go to school, you can get a real job and I'll be there to care for them when they get home. It's the best option for us all.'

Although Gally's main reason for suggesting the move was to help the young family, it would also benefit her. She was often lonely now and Polly and Ellen spent many evenings out, and Ellen was already courting. It wouldn't be long before she was completely alone and that was not something she was anticipating with any degree of pleasure.

Within a week, it had been arranged and the two women moved their meagre collections of belongings further up the

254

Severn valley and settled into the two cottages. The river flowed just feet away from their front doors and Gally woke each morning to the rushing and gurgling of the water, and the knowledge that her childhood home, Cancoed, was less than a mile away on the other side of the river. Her life had indeed come full circle.

These latter years were full of quiet contentment, as young Peg took up residence in the second bedroom of her cottage. Gally enjoyed the company of her young grandchildren, especially in the evenings, and – once Peg left home to begin work as a live-in maid – Marie took her place, and a few years later she was replaced by Davy. Her first grandson had always had a special place in her heart and, as they spent more time together, the bond between them strengthened and the two became inseparable. There had never been any more news of Tommy and, although she worried, Gally tried to remain hopeful that one day he would turn up out of the blue. Each night she continued to leave a candle in the window.

In 1934, Gally turned seventy and on her birthday, after her grandsons had set off for school, she began her preparations for a visit to town. The evening before, she had filled the tin bath with hot water and eased her old bones in gently, relishing the warmth all around her. After soaping her body, she had washed her long white hair, giving it a final rinse with vinegar laced water before towelling it dry in front of the fire. Now she brushed out her hair – much thinner than it had been in her youth – and twisted it tightly in a knot at the back of her head, securing the bun with just a few hair pins. She took out one of her Sunday dresses, a new pair of lisle stockings and added her chapel coat and hat. This was a special day, and it was important to her to look her best. She looked at the little watch that Sarah Jane and the children had bought her for her birthday, tightened the leather strap and headed for the door. She walked more slowly now and it was a steep climb to reach the lane but, although slightly out of breath, she made it minutes before the rumble of a motor could be heard.

There was now a daily bus that wound its way into town in the morning and returned up the valley in the afternoon. This new form of transport had quite transformed her life, and when old Dolly had literally dropped in her tracks, there had been no talk of another pony and the wooden trap was now slowly disintegrating behind the house. Normally, Gally would take the bus once a week to collect her shopping and visit the library, but this was an extra visit and one that deserved to be free from of distractions.

Sitting upright in her seat, she watched the fields and hedges flash by, her heart quickening at the thought of what lay ahead. She opened her small handbag and checked the contents of the brown envelope again. Inside sat her buff-coloured pension book. Today she was entitled to draw an old-age pension.

Getting off the bus at Market Hall, she walked along to the Post Office and joined the small queue of people. She nodded and smiled at those she knew and soon she was at the front of the line and looking through the wire mesh screen at the lady assistant.

'How can I help? What would you like?'

Pushing forward her pension book, Gally spoke up proudly. 'I have come to collect my pension payment, please.'

'Of course,' replied the young lady and, picking up a heavy stamp, she pushed it down onto the ink-soaked sponge before forcefully stamping the counterfoil of the first page in the book. The other half was ripped out, filed away in a heavy wooden drawer and then the money – two florins and a shilling – was pushed across the counter. The whole procedure took less than a minute.

Gally scrabbled to pick up the money with arthritic fingers and moved aside to put it away in her purse before leaving the building. Flushed with success and amazed at how easy the whole process had been, she laughed out loud and headed for the baker's shop. They would have doughnuts for tea tonight.

*

As the bus rattled its way back up the hill, she thought back to John Jenkins, who had first introduced her to the concept of socialism, and to all the speeches she had read by David Lloyd George. How things had changed in her lifetime; if only her parents had been able to get this kind of help in their later years, their lives would have been so much easier and they may not have died so early. There had been so many arguments with Thomas, but she knew how much this regular payment would help old people like her and now she could show her support for socialism without fear of it leading to raised voices.

The small payment of only five shillings a week made a huge difference to her life, and her days could now be spent in her garden and kitchen, growing and preserving fruit and vegetables, baking and cooking nourishing meals to share with the family. Her presence at home meant that Sarah Jane had returned to a full-time job at the hospital, as Gally was there to look after the children when they returned from school each day. They would rush to her door, hurrying inside to see what was waiting for them, a tasty cawl or hot pie with delicious crumbly pastry.

Sunday chapel services were an unquestioned part of the week. Chapel attendance was not only for religious observance, it was also a social event; a coming together of the community. For Gally and Davy, it was about the music and the singing; they would stand, side by side, in the pews, and let the old familiar tunes pour from them in sheer enjoyment. As the family would make their way home after the Sunday service, they would often continue their singing as they walked down the narrow lanes.

There were many special days bound up with the Nonconformist chapel congregation. As well as the major services of the religious calendar, there were festivals of preaching, when the enormous chapels of Llanidloes would be filled with people wanting to hear the sermons from the eminent preachers of the day. Due to their popularity, tickets had to be purchased in advance. The chapel deacons would be seen with big smiles as they counted the admission money.

In the autumn of 1936, Gally looked into her savings tin and withdrew sufficient money to buy three tickets, three seated places for the forthcoming festival. She bought one for herself, one for her daughter, Ellen – who was the most devout of her children – and one for Davy, because there would be wonderful hymn-singing, both before and after the preaching.

On the day of the festival, the three of them dressed in their Sunday best and walked down, through Penygreen, to the chapel on China Street. Here they joined the long queue of people, all waiting for the doors to be opened. There was a palpable air of excitement and anticipation, and she held tightly to Davy's hand, much to his embarrassment, at twelve years of age. As she looked around and smiled at those she knew, she turned to her grandson with a smile.

'This is going to be a wonderful occasion, Davy. You must listen to every word and, just maybe, you will still remember all this when you are grown up and, who knows, maybe far from here.'

He nodded, eager more for the singing than the preaching, but he hadn't wanted to upset Gally by saying so. At last, the huge doors were opened and the eager crowds filed in, taking their places, one by one, in the high-backed pews. By two-thirty, there was not a spare inch left in the building: extra chairs had been placed in the aisles and every seat was taken.

Finally, the door opened from the vestry, and out proceeded a group of three ministers and many more elders of the chapel, all dressed in black, long-tailed coats. They took their places behind the pulpit in the raised seats, reminding Davy of the line of crows that he often saw on the barn roof. In the heavy silence of the chapel, the organ burst into sound, a sound so powerful and beautiful compared to the old harmonium, which was all they had in the little chapel at Glan Hafren.

After several rousing hymns, the congregation sat, and silence fell. Close as everyone was to each other, there was no shuffling or fidgeting, only a communal desire to hear the words of the speaker that day, Dr Elvet Lewis. Gally had read in her newspapers about this man. He had come from humble beginnings in Wales but had begun his preaching at a very early age before attending college and going into the ministry. He had a long and prestigious career and was, at this time, minister at King's Cross Chapel in London. It was a rare occasion for him to be in Wales, and Gally had been looking forward to this day for weeks.

This charismatic preacher held forth for nearly three hours on the topic of 'New wine in old bottles'. His bilingualism, training and his devout belief in the teaching of Jesus enabled him to preach completely without notes, and to move from Welsh to English and back again, with no faltering. The congregation was spellbound; this was one of Wales' greatest orators and he caught them in a fine web of poetry, religious fervour and drama. Such was his presence that the physical discomfort of the hard pews went unnoticed.

When he finally fell silent and stepped down from the pulpit, the organist struck the first notes of 'Calon Lân' and the congregation stood as one. If the singing had been excellent before, it now reached new heights, filling the building with powerful emotion and a beauty and clarity of sound. This was their response to Elvet Lewis, their gratitude and their commitment.

It was late in the afternoon when they made their way slowly from the chapel and turned for home. They walked slowly, saying little, tired with the heightened emotions of the day.

It was Davy who broke the silence. 'Thank you, Gally. Thank you for taking me. I didn't understand it all but I shall never forget it. I felt as if he was talking just to me, as if he could see into me.'

Smiling, she replied, 'I'm sure everyone inside the chapel felt like that, Davy. It's a gift he has. He makes everyone feel that they matter.'

'Well, we do all matter, don't we?'

'We do, Davy. But life will take you to places where it will seem that you matter less than others. At those times, you just remember today. You think about the way Elvet Lewis made you feel, as if you mattered. You are as good as anyone, but not better than anyone, and nor is anyone else better than you. You remember both those things, Davy.'

Epilogue

MY FATHER, DAVY, was fourteen when his beloved Gally died, and I can think of no better way to end the telling of this lady's life than to share with you the story as he told it to me.

In the last months of her life, Gally had grown weaker, her heart was failing and her energy had declined. Davy was by now working as a farmhand across the river at Cancoed, Gally's childhood home, and now owned by her nephew. Each day, he would leave the little bedroom in Gally's cottage and follow the river down to the first narrow bridge where he would cross the swirling water and climb the bank, crossing the fields until he reached the house. Here, Uncle Dick would give him his jobs for the day and he would work outside in all weathers with little to protect him from the wind and rain but an old sack tied across his shoulders. When the day's chores were done, he would retrace his steps back to the cottage and eat the meal she would have prepared for him. Then it was his turn to repay her and fill the coal buckets, chop the morning sticks in readiness for the next day's fire. Gally no longer had the breath to sing but often in the evenings, while she read her newspaper, he would sing the old hymns to her, and so they would pass an hour or two before bed.

As autumn turned to winter, the trees lost their bright

colours and the days grew shorter and colder. Gally, too, became weaker and less inclined to leave her bed. Sarah Jane would visit her in the morning, and again when she returned from work, caring for her mother as best she could. It seemed that Gally had a strong sense that her days were numbered, and she began to give away small keepsakes to her children and grandchildren when they visited. She asked for Tommy's picture to be moved to her bedroom and could often be heard mumbling away to him. Sitting in her bed one evening, listening to Davy by her side, her eyes crinkled with pleasure at his singing and, as he finished, she pressed his hand before whispering, 'My Bible, Davy. It will be yours after I am gone. I want you to have it.'

She had little of consequence to leave to anyone but he knew how much it meant that she wanted him to have this precious book.

Returning home from a long day at work just a few days later, Davy had to walk along the lane, as the riverside path was too icy and dangerous. He turned the corner and began to walk down the hill towards the cottages, when he saw a light moving along the path. He had no need of a lantern, he knew his way in the dark, and the moon was light enough. He stood and watched the glowing light as it zigzagged along the path, hovered in front of him, then passed by and disappeared into the distance. Had it been summer, he thought it might have been a firefly, but never in December.

As he reached the door of Gally's cottage, he found his mother there, tears in her eyes. 'Oh Davy, you are too late. Gally died just a few minutes ago.'

Sadly, Tommy never returned, was never seen or heard of by the family again and all my efforts to trace him came to nothing.

Acknowledgements

FROM THE FIRST moment of finding out about my great-grandmother, Margaret, I was compelled to write the story. From the tiny seed first planted at Gregynog that sunny afternoon, grew a deep fondness for this lady, a sympathy with all that she had suffered and huge admiration for her inner strength.

I read many books about Welsh history, about life in Montgomeryshire, its places and people, and would like to pay tribute to those I especially found helpful: *Sex, Sects and Society, Pain and Pleasure* by Russell Davies, *Llanidloes Town and Parish – An Introduction* by E. Ronald Morris, *A Municipal History of Llanidloes* (1908) by Ernest Richmond Horsfall Turner, *The History of the Zion United Reform Church* by D. Maxwell Lewis, *Suffrage Movement in the Newtown Area and Beyond* by Newtown Local History Group, 'Gregynog 1880–1920', dissertation by Rachel Jones MA, in *The Montgomeryshire Collection*, Volume 30.

I would like to thank the National Library of Wales for making available the Gregynog Estate Records; reading these proved to be a much more emotional experience than I had expected, as I held in my hands the evidence of their small wages and then compared them to the rent for their homes. There was little left to live off when the latter had been paid.

I owe enormous gratitude to Mary Oldham, Librarian at

Gregynog Hall, for patiently answering my questions, taking time to give me a guided tour of the house, explaining the layout of the building as it would have been in the late 19th century and reading my manuscript to make sure that I hadn't made any errors concerning the house and its history. I would also like to thank the present Lord Joicey, who also answered my questions and was most helpful. Also, Rhiannon Williams from the Tregynon Heritage Hub for sharing many articles and photographs.

At the mid-point of writing the book I attended a writing course at Tŷ Newydd, run by Literature Wales. The course was entitled, 'Writing Historical Fiction', and I was so fortunate to have as my tutors Louise Walsh and Phil Carradice, both of whom were so supportive and made me promise to finish the book and send it to publishers. They will probably never know how much their encouragement meant to me at that time. I am profoundly grateful to Lefi Gruffudd at Y Lolfa for accepting my book, and Eirian Jones, my editor, for all the work that has since been done to reach publication.

I owe much of my love for Wales and its history and culture to my father, David Davies, and I am so grateful to him and my aunt, Marie Roberts, for sharing their memories of Gally and their childhood with me. I am so sad that my much loved father passed away at the end of 2021 and wasn't able to see the book in its finished form; he was however enormously proud of the fact that I had written it. He and my aunt brought my great-grandmother to life, and the more I came to know her, the more she took hold of me. To my dear friends, Jenny and Louise, thank you for all your support and interest and willingness to read and reread my manuscript. It was greatly appreciated.

Lastly and most importantly, my thanks and love to my husband John who remained steadfast in his conviction that I would finish the book and it would be published. There were many moments along the journey when I may well have given up without your belief in me. Not to forget the tea and the wine.

Also from Y Lolfa:

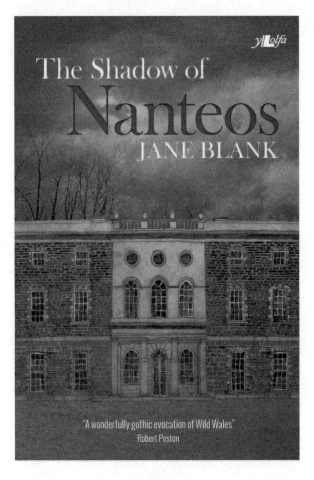

£8.99

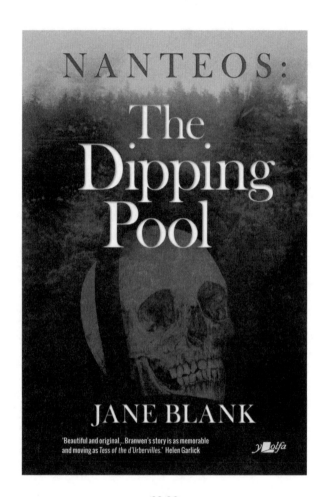

NANTEOS:

The
Dipping
Pool

JANE BLANK

'Beautiful and original... Branwen's story is as memorable
and moving as *Tess of the d'Urbervilles*.' Helen Garlick

y Lolfa

£9.99

"A family history powerfully reimagined as an absorbing and moving fiction."

In The Vale
Sam Adams

y Lolfa

£9.99

Ask for a print quote!
www.ylolfa.com